EASY MONEY

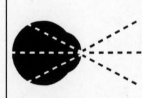

This Large Print Book carries the
Seal of Approval of N.A.V.H.

EASY MONEY

FRANK RODERUS

THORNDIKE PRESS

A part of Gale, Cengage Learning

GALE
CENGAGE Learning®

Farmington Hills, Mich • San Francisco • New York • Waterville, Maine
Meriden, Conn • Mason, Ohio • Chicago

GALE
CENGAGE Learning®

LIBRARY OF CONGRESS CATALOGING-IN-PUBLICATION DATA

Roderus, Frank, 1942–
  Easy money / by Frank Roderus. — Large print edition.
    pages ; cm. — (Thorndike Press large print western)
    ISBN 978-1-4104-6787-4 (hardcover) — ISBN 1-4104-6787-2 (hardcover)
    1. Large type books. I. Title.
  PS3568.O346E17 2014
  813'.54—dc23   2014016892

Published in 2014 by arrangement with Hartline Literary Agency

Printed in Mexico
1 2 3 4 5 6 7 18 17 16 15 14

This one for Melisse and Franklin

CHAPTER 1

Chic came to work for the OX5 the same day I did, though that was strictly coincidental. The outfit was running four thousand head of two-year-old steers on leased grass in the Cherokee Strip, growing them out to market weight when they would be driven north into Kansas for rail shipment to the buyers back east. The brand belonged to O. X. Horton, called Ox Horton by those of us who didn't know him. I say this because neither me nor any of the other boys ever laid eyes on the man. The manager of this particular bunch was a stiff-necked teetotaler named Willard Hammond, and it was to him that everyone looked for their pay. Come to think of it, I don't even know where this Horton lived, though he must have had a power of stock cows tucked away somewhere to be feeding all those young steers onto the Strip for fattening.

Anyway, I wandered into the OX5 headquarters camp from the south, coming up from Texas and being sort of loose at the time and a bit low on cash. I was drawn there by the smoke of noontime cooking at the dugout they had scratched into a hillside, and I determined to stay when Hammond allowed that he was low on men and would pay twenty-five dollars a month. That seemed a hair on the low side but I didn't know what the going rate was in that country, and it sure was twenty-five dollars better than nothing. So I ate and nodded to the other boys and told the man I would stay a while.

Chic came by that same evening, I would guess for pretty much the same reasons. He rode in from the north on a nicely made but much-traveled yellow horse. You could see right off that he was loose jointed and likable. He had no sooner stepped out of the saddle than he was smiling and nodding to everyone and sticking his hand out for it to be shook. "I'm Chic Robertson and hidey-do." That sort of thing.

I've always envied people who can be so free and easy among strangers. Me, I tend to hang back and keep my mouth shut around folks I don't know, and some accuse me of being standoffish, which I do not intend at all. But a person can't hardly run

8

around explaining that to total strangers.

No one would ever call Chic Robertson standoffish, and he had that kind of good looks and open smile that people can take to too. Curly yellow hair and real pale blue eyes and laugh wrinkles hiding in the deep tan of his face. He was maybe a couple years older than me, call it twenty-four or -five, and tall and broad-shouldered but with a horsebacker's slim build and a smooth step as light as that of a kit fox.

When he came around to me, Chic shook and told me his name and I told him mine — Bert Felloe — knowing he would do like most everyone else I'd ever met and soon be calling me Fella or Fellow the way most folks will call a colored man "boy" or a Mexican "Pancho." But Chic never did. He looked me in the eye and said, "Pleased to meet you, Bert," and it was Bert from then on as far as he was concerned.

After supper Hammond called Chic aside and they had a little talk, and pretty soon Chic nodded and it seemed a safe bet that the outfit was no longer shorthanded.

Come morning the manager assigned Chic and me each a four-horse string and as we were both newcomers to the pack it seemed the natural thing that he would pair us off for the day's work as well.

There was not much to a job like that, certainly nothing like the thorns and the sweat of busting wild ones out of the Brasada down home or even the dust and the sweat of nursemaiding a herd along a trail. All we had to do was ride a circle around the herd — call it a thirty-mile swing — pushing any drifting OX5 steers back in toward the middle and turning back anything else that might want to drift onto our grass.

I roped out a deep-chested sorrel that looked like he might have some staying power, and Chic took a ewe-necked paint horse that had a mean look in his eye but had a tough and rangy look about him as well. Neither horse offered to do any real serious bucking, which I took to be a good sign. It has been my experience that if there is a really bad horse in my string, I'll manage to find him with the first swing of my loop.

Another pair of riders started a circle to the west, while Chic and I rode east. Three other boys and Hammond would be wandering around in the center of things, checking watering places for bogged steers and looking for screwworms to doctor and whatever else might be needed. There were also a couple younguns who handled the horses, one during the day and the other kid at night. The cooking seemed to be a catch-as-catch-can affair with most of the burden falling on the day wrangler.

We hadn't gone five miles nor seen a dozen OX5 animals before Chic leaned over and poked me in the arm.

"Look there, Bert. A dollar says I put a rope on him before you do." He was pointing toward a patchy-coated little prairie wolf that was skulking in the grass not too far away.

"I don't guess I have a dollar to put up," I told him.

"Hell, neither do I," he said with a grin. "Payday."

He didn't wait for an answer. He let out a yelp and threw the steel to that spotted horse and away they went, Chic standing up in his stirrups with the wind in his teeth while he shook a loop into his coil.

Well, I wasn't going to sit around waiting to be beat. I roweled that sorrel good and hard and went kiting after them like I didn't still have a circle to make on that horse. I gave a holler loud enough to match Chic's and stood swaying with the bunch and drive of the sorrel's muscles while the crisp morning air whistled past my ears, and damn but it was fun.

The little wolf saw us coming and began to scamper uphill. He jinked to the right as he neared the top of the rise, and Chic had to rein his pony to follow. I leaned into my right stirrup and the sorrel swung with the shift of my weight. That cut the angle a bit so that I picked up some ground.

Chic's paint had the idea now, though, and he was closer. The pony was giving it all he had and moved in behind and just to the left of the wolf. That little animal was running scared and belly down.

Chic dropped his reins and took a couple twirls to open his loop. He threw it hard and true and snatched his slack most as soon as the loop had left his hand. Even so, the loop sailed smack over the wolf's head and the little critter leaped through before the rope could close. It dodged to the left and bolted smack under the neck of that spotted pony.

I was right behind them at the time. There wasn't time for any fancy twirling or even to think about it. As the wolf came alongside the left of my sorrel I whipped my loop over and down. It was sheer luck, but with my short, brush-country rope and the little bitty loop I'd always been taught to use, I managed to snag that old wolf. My loop went over his head and drew up around his hindquarters.

The sorrel slid to a stop and began backing away, and the wolf commenced to yip and holler. He threw himself around and about and up and down, snarling and yapping the whole while, until he began to raise a dust out of that thick, bluestem grass. My pony was steady backing away trying to keep that rope tight, but of course there wasn't enough weight on the other end to keep it really tight. The wolf couldn't have been caught more than two seconds before it slipped free and was running again, tail tucked and it really churning.

I looked at Chic and he was sitting doubled over on the paint, just laughing to beat all billy hell.

"I guess you might call that a tie," I offered.

"A tie? I should say we won't," Chic protested, still laughing. "You got 'im fair and square, Bert. But did you ever see anything so funny?" He leaned forward another few inches and swept a hand under his pony's neck, jiggering the sweaty animal a little. "Little devil went right underneath me, he did. If I'd had any sense I'd've grabbed 'is tail. Then you'd've owed me a dollar 'stead of the other way around." He grinned. "Sure was worth it, though. Damn me if it wasn't, Bert."

We got down and loosened our cinches and let the horses blow for a cigarette's worth of time before we went on.

I guess I might have been willing to keep quiet about how we had used those circle horses when they had work to do, especially as I didn't know this outfit and didn't know how they would take to tomfoolery on company time and company horseflesh, but not Chic.

That night he regaled the whole crowd with a blow-by-blow account of the whole thing, puffing it up until every one of those boys was laughing along with him and him giving the impression that I was some kind of trick artist with a rope, and if Hammond ever said a word of caution to him about it, I never heard anything of it.

Once started that way we stayed paired, and I soon found that old Chic was always ready to pause for some skylarking, whether trying to rope something or race something or investigate a patch of brush we hadn't crashed through before or whatever. There was always time for a little fun to break the monotony. And nerveless? That boy never gave a thought to what might be underfoot next. Once he set spurs to his horse he wouldn't quit until he'd busted over or clear through whatever was in front of him. I'd thought we had some wild-riding boys down in the brush country, but that was before I met Chic. I stayed with him, but I was steady wondering when I would be needed there beside him for the purpose of picking up the pieces.

In spite of all that we made a pretty fair pair, for Chic didn't seem to know what anyone meant if he said he was tired. No matter what we had just finished doing, he was always ready to go do something else, especially if it involved something he considered fun or invigorating, like a top-speed run over new country at night. Put the wind in his ears, and that boy was happy. And he always seemed surprised when his horse would come up sweating and trembling from overwork; Chic was still ready to go, so the horse should be too.

He was a pretty fair hand with a rope, too, and we spent a deal of time trying to prove to each other that our way of handling a catch rope was better than the other's.

Chic used a long, rather light rope, maybe sixty feet of it, that he called a lariat, which I believe was the first I'd ever heard that term. He threw big loops and dallied the free end around the horn of his saddle. He had wrapped the neck of the horn with

15

rawhide to give the rope something to bite into, and when he had a particularly stout something in his loop, he would slip his dally to give it more rope and sort of ease it down like a man playing a big fish on fight cord. That lightweight rope of his could not have taken the strain of really busting one down, but the way he played his dallies Chic made sure that it didn't have to.

My rope, of course, was much more stout and twenty-five feet long. There was no free end to it, there being a horn loop worked into the end so that it was tied more or less permanently to the apple on my saddle. And there was no toying with something once I put my loop onto it. As soon as that loop tightened it was brace-and-be-damned boys, for something had to give.

As for which method was better, I guess in truth you could say it was something of a stand-off. That big loop of his could be laid around almost anything, but it being so big, the animal could shake it or run through it more frequent. Nothing is likely to shake out of my little loops, but they were easier to dodge and maybe a little harder to throw true, so I missed a lot more throws than Chic did. I guess you would have to say that the differences pretty much evened things out and brought it all down to a matter of preference.

And as for how we stacked up one against the other. Well, after a couple weeks I sure was hoping Chic was keeping track of who owed how many dollars to whom, for I was getting purely confused.

It was his way to get himself a fun idea, holler "a dollar says I can . . ." and be gone after it before I had time to say aye, nay, or maybe.

I got him one day, though. Chic had pulled to a stop to hook a knee over his horn and roll a smoke. I wandered ahead a little ways to see what was on the other side of the next little rise.

There on the hard-baked, dry ground was a scuffed and dusty patch that showed some horse tracks in the dust and a big old dead rattlesnake that some pony had chopped up fairly recent.

I moved my horse in beside the dead thing and dropped my loop onto the ground. It took a little maneuvering but after a bit I was able to tug that snake into a neat enough pile that I could get the loop to close on it tight enough to pick the thing up in my rope.

I looked back and here came Chic ambling up toward me with his knee still hooked over his saddle horn, hands in his pockets,

17

and a curl of cigarette smoke bumping into his hat brim. He did look relaxed.

"A dollar says I can rope a snake before you," I told him.

"Huh?" He cocked his head and peered at me with one eye, the other being shut against the smoke.

I repeated what I'd said, and he sort of grinned.

Well, I up and hefted that snake out of the grass so he could see it for the first time and as luck would have it the tail fell out of the rope so that the thing must've looked like it was wiggling.

Chic's eyes got wide, and I flipped the end of my rope up and over, right toward him. The snake fell out of the loop and sailed into the air in his direction.

Chic ducked and the chestnut he was riding that day jumped, and for a minute there old Chic was all feet and hands and each one of the fourteen of them was clutching for leather. Him and that horse raised quite a dust and when they ended up they were about fifty yards further away and Chic was sideways in his saddle. He still had the one stirrup, though, and had a good grip on the horn.

He got himself back into a proper seat and picked his hat out of the grass where it had landed and eyed me from the distance while he rolled and lighted another smoke. Finally he rode back up to me.

"It was already dead, wasn't it?"

"Uh huh." I guess I did snicker a bit.

Chic looked at me and then at that dead snake and then back at me. He started to grin and the next thing we both of us were laughing and giggling and guffawing like a pair of fools. "I — God, Bert. A dead snake." He laughed and shook his head.

We had ridden about a half mile further when he turned in the saddle and told me, "Guess I owe you a dollar, Bert."

"Uh huh," I told him. "Payday."

He shook his head again and chuckled to himself.

CHAPTER 2

Come payday I learned something about Chic. Quick as he was to make a wager, he was just as quick to forget a debt. He hadn't any more idea than me of who owed how much to whom. And from the way he threw his head and laughed when I asked him about it, he must have cared even less than I did about that little detail.

What we decided to do about it was to declare it a draw from then on. Which did not stop Chic from offering his dollar bets about anything or about nothing.

We were partnered out there in that open grass for a couple more months before I ever saw Chic Robertson be serious about anything. But when I did, I sure was glad to see it.

What happened was that we were on a circle one bright and puff-cloud day, and I had myself some trouble.

Chic had drifted off to the side to poke

through a tangled old plum thicket where we had several times bounced little bunches of fiddle-footed steers that might've slipped off the OX5 area if they hadn't been started back south.

I rode ahead to turn aside a group of five wandering bovines coming down onto our grass from wherever it was they belonged. They were still too far away to read their brands, but I could see flaps of cut skin dangling down off their chests and the OX5 did not use a dewlap mark, just the brand and earmarks. Whatever they were, they belonged elsewhere. I bumped the hard-headed brute I was riding a good one with my spurs and went to head them and start them back north.

The black horse I was using that day was a fine-looking animal, but he was strictly skin deep. There wasn't the first bit of good sense under any part of his hide, and he was stumble-footed too. Once I'd gotten to know him I used him only for riding circle, since he couldn't be trusted inside the herd where there was more likelihood of having to rope or cut so we could doctor our steers. There really wasn't enough endurance in him for circle riding either, but I'd kept hoping he would turn up wind-broken some day so I would've had a reason to knock him off my string without it looking like I was a complainer. Because of that I always rode him plenty hard when I did have to use him, and that might account for why we didn't get along so well. He didn't trust me a lick more than I trusted him.

Anyway, I shoved him into a hard run at those five strays and pretty soon I could see that the beeves were four stock cows wearing a curlicued Mexican brand of some sort and one elderly bull with a 41 on his off flank. I cut in front of them and went to spin the black to face them when he jiggered on me.

I was paying attention to the bovines and had already shifted my weight with the quick spin I was expecting to be making. The black, though, buggered off in the other direction, and before I knew what was happening I was riding on just one side of that horse. I'd lost my left stirrup entirely and wound up with both legs on the right of the horse and my free hand clutched with a grip like a deep-woods tick on my saddle horn.

I cussed a little and snatched at the black's mouth to teach him some manners. The devil threw his head and when he did he stumbled. Maybe he had seen what was coming and I messed up his balance. I'll never know for sure about that, but I do know that for a few seconds there all my attention had been on the horse.

Without any warning at all, there was a blur of motion just under my feet and a loud whoosh of air. It sounded like an oversize cough. And then the horse screamed.

I looked down and there was that 41 bull with his left horn painted a gaudy, bloody red, his dull yellow eyes walled and frothing slobber on his muzzle. I will say that I had sense enough to be damn well scared.

The bull hooked that left horn at the black again, and I tried to scramble over to the other side of the horse. The impact of that sharp, stubby horn going in the second time was enough that I could feel the shock of it carry clear through the flesh of the black gelding. Then we were going down.

I tried to boost myself clear. Damn, but I tried. But without that left stirrup I had nothing to push against. I slipped down along the left side of the black's barrel just as he squealed again and fell hard to his left, helped no doubt by the driving power of the bull.

For long seconds there the whole world was a confusion of dust and the screams of the horse and the smell of blood and dirt close in my nostrils. I felt another distant impact, and the horse stopped its screaming. It occurred to me finally that even though I was trying to roll or crawl or scramble out of there, I wasn't going anywhere. I was lying mostly underneath a horse that was already dead or so close to it as to make no difference.

From where I lay I couldn't see over past the bulk of the horse, but I could hear plenty. The scraping and snorting said plain enough that that renegade bull was still there, pawing at the ground and swelling his neck and feeling plenty proud of himself.

I raised up to peer across toward him, and that was a mistake. I caught a glimpse of the top of his head and he must have caught a glimpse of mine. He bellowed and charged again.

His left horn slashed deep into the belly of the horse for the third time. The force of it was enough to shift the whole eight or nine hundred pounds of dead horse, grinding me along underneath it.

The bull might have gotten its feet tangled in the legs of the horse, but for whatever reason it stumbled forward and half rolled across to my side of the black. I could actually hear the hide tear as the horn was ripped free. The bull was panting and wild-eyed. The left horn was a dark, bloody mess, and more blood was splashed across its

24

chest and forequarters.

Me, I was scared. The only limb I had free for use was my right arm. The left had gotten trapped under the horse when the beast was shifted. Lordy, I laid there not daring to hardly breathe and listened to my heartbeat pound in my ears, loud as the drums in a parade. If I showed any hint of motion, that crazy son of a bitch would be coming again.

I have no idea how long I hung suspended in time there. It could not have been for very long, I guess, but at the moment it seemed like this exact instant was all there ever had been or all there ever would be in the whole of time. It had no beginning and seemed that it could have only one end. As soon as I moved, the bull would slash again. My eyes felt dry and gritty from staring at that bull, but I was afraid to blink.

Of a sudden the bull's head raised and it wheeled away, its hind feet just missing stepping on me. I could hear hooves coming at a hard run. The bull trotted forward a little ways with short, stiff-legged steps. It lowered its head and snorted.

I turned my head. It was Chic, of course. He was up in the stirrups and coming hard.

The bull swung its head from side to side. Its tail jerked upright and it wheeled back toward me and the dead horse.

I knew what it was going to do, all right. It was going to run. And on the way it would take one more swipe of the horn at and into this thing it had conquered. And there was not one damn thing I could do about it.

Those long, heavy muscles bunched, and the thing began charging again, straight toward me. If I'd had any sense I suppose I would've closed my eyes, but I could not. I lay there and watched it come. Watched the nostrils flare. Watched the thick neck drop and that left horn turn lower to cut and tear.

And I saw Chic's big, sloppy loop smack down across the head, catch the upraised right horn and pull the beast off balance. I could feel a gush of hot, wet air being expelled from those wide nostrils as the thing passed over me like a cloud of death. I felt one sharp stab of pain as a churning hoof grazed down against my ribs. And then it was gone.

I don't remember for sure but I believe I was sobbing just a little.

A moment later the bright light of the sky was blotted out by an upside-down look at a serious and subdued Chic Robertson.

I swallowed hard and took in a shuddering breath.

I winked at Chic. He grinned and was himself again. I hadn't hardly recognized him with that grim look on him.

"You shouldn't ought to lay down on the job, Bert. It ain't right t' make me do all the work."

"Tell me about it." Now that I had time to notice it, it hurt like hell to talk. Or to breathe, for that matter. I was under considerable weight, being mostly blanketed by dead horse. Thank goodness he *was* dead, though. Any thrashing or wallowing around by a live horse in such a predicament would have had my ribs snapping like so many eggshells, and maybe more important stuff as well.

"I s'pose you'll want me to get this thing off you," Chic ventured. He was hunkered down beside me. He might have sounded casual about it, but I knew that what he was doing was looking things over to see how he could do this without causing more damage than he was preventing.

"When it's convenient," I told him.

"Uh huh." He studied on it some more, got up and walked around to look from fresh angles, finally came back and sat on the shoulder of the dead black. He grinned down at me. "Know what I think?"

"Nope."

"I think it cain't be done."

"Nice of you to be so encouraging."

"Yeah. Seriously, Bert, there's no way I can drag this thing off'n you without doing who-knows-what more harm. Not without a tripod or some such way to get a straight-up lift."

"All right," I told him. It was commencing to hurt pretty good, and I guess I was sweating kind of heavy. Chic undid my bandanna and gave it to me so I could mop my face when I wanted.

"Tooley and Greason shouldn't be too far," he said. "I'll find them and shag on back here quick as I can."

"Okay." He was right, of course. There just wasn't anything else to do. "You know where to find me when you get done flitting around."

Chic got up and crunched away. He was back in a minute with a Colt's revolver, one of the ordinary kind that used cap and loose powder, though lately a lot of boys had been having them converted to use cartridges. He laid that where I could reach it with my one free hand. "In case you get to fretting."

"Thanks." It would be a comfort, too. I'd already been getting visions of that bull coming back.

I don't know how long Chic was gone. I

know that it seemed a long, hot, dry time, and I was awfully glad when I heard horses coming. Chic and the other boys rode close and sat there grinning down at me. Lordy, but those horses and riders did look tall standing over me there.

"I see you didn't get so bored you decided to leave," Chic said.

"Too busy," I said. "Counting clouds." There wasn't a one in the sky just then.

They swung down and talked it over, chatting away among the three of them as if I wasn't there. There was no point in three men trying to pick up a dead horse, but they tried it anyway. They got nowhere.

Harmon Tooley — whom I began to suspect was not too bright — suggested they take the black by the legs and roll it over. Fortunately the others dissuaded him. The only place they could've rolled the damn thing would have been onto my head and shoulders, of which I could not greatly approve.

What they ended up doing was to use Tooley's horse — the steadiest of the three we had — to stand beside the black. They ran ropes across Harmon's saddle and pulled from the far side with the other two horses. That way they got some upward lift, though it was a bit rough on both the horse and the saddle being used for the purpose. But it worked. There was enough lift and shift that with a little help from Harmon I was able to wiggle out of there.

"Jee-zus!" I said. And I did not mean it in any sacrilegious manner either.

I don't believe I'd ever before felt so light nor so free nor so cool. Do you know, it had been awfully *hot* under that horse. I think I'd minded that more than the weight, which I'd almost gotten used to as long as I hadn't tried to move.

I had a few bad moments there when I found that I couldn't feel anything in my legs. They seemed to be working all right, I mean I could bend them and everything, but I couldn't feel them and would not have wanted to try standing on them. Then the circulation got to working normally again, and I found they'd just been asleep. For a while there it was like being tickled half to death with needle tips. I got to rubbing at them — and I guess groaning some — and Harmon rubbed and so did Chic and Clyde Greason and pretty soon they were back toward normal.

Other than that and a little soreness along the ribs, there didn't seem to be a thing wrong with me.

"I s'pose you know you're a pretty lucky

fella, Fella," Clyde said.

"If you say so, it must be true," I told him. "If it hadn't been for old Chic here I'd've been a dead fella, that's for sure."

That brought their eyebrows up a notch.

"You mean he didn't tell you what he did?" So I told them. And Chic, not being overly shy, sat there and lapped up some nice words about himself. Why, I got so carried away I even paid him some compliments on his roping and never once mentioned how inferior his dally style was.

CHAPTER 3

We were doing okay there and I had saved eighteen dollars out of my pay — largely because there was practically nothing to spend it on at the few stores we could reach in a reasonable riding distance — when that particular employment played out on us.

We had gone down the week before to a store run by an Osage named Watson and had relaxed a little. Visited with the mulatto girl who did business in a brush arbor near the store and bought clean shirts and a bottle or two. Nothing rowdy. Anyway, Chic carried a jug back with him in his saddle pockets, which is something I would say probably half the boys did when they got the chance.

This particular day we'd been working in the herd and had had kind of a rougher than usual time of it. The rains seemed to be past now and the pockets of standing water were beginning to disappear. Steers that had gotten accustomed to watering in certain places didn't want to give them up. They were wading into the gooey slop that had been pond bottoms a month before, searching for drinking water and finding mostly mud.

That led to a good many of the stupid things getting bogged belly-deep, and while it was possible sometimes to drop a rope on one and yank him out, you mostly had to get in there with him and dig him loose, one man doing that while the other kept a steady pull with horse and rope. That helped pull the steer free quicker and also cut down on the likelihood of one turning around and poking a horn into the man working afoot. For a steer has no sense of gratitude and after being aggravated by the bog so long, one is often ready to fight with the first thing that comes to hand. Or to horn, as the case may be.

And I did say they are stupid, didn't I? Too damned often you can work for an hour digging a beef out of a bog and set it loose only to have the silly damn thing decide then that it's still thirsty and march right back into the same bog.

Anyhow, this day we got in a bit late, pretty tired and well greased with a layer of gummy, drying mud, which does nothing on a hot evening to make a man feel cooler or more comfortable.

We pulled the gear off our horses and turned the animals out with the *remuda.* Neither one of us felt much like lugging saddles back to the dugout, so we just left them where they'd dropped.

I was admiring the rich, bright smell of boiled coffee for quite a ways before we reached the dugout and was wondering what they might have cooked to go with it.

We stopped outside to strip off our muddy clothes, since the roof of the dugout was not quite high enough to permit standing fully erect. You had to crouch just a bit.

Chic was ahead of me at the door. He peeled his shirt off and started to kick out of his boots and called, "Somebody inside hand out me'n Bert's warbags, will ya?"

A minute later the ramrod, Willard Hammond, stuck his head out. He tossed me my bag, but he hefted Chic's and sort of bounced it on his fingertips. The clank of a bottle hitting against something was just as plain as anything could be. Hammond bounced the bag a second time and sort of grinned to himself when he heard that telltale sound again.

Now I will have to admit that it was not hard to figure out what was in that bag. For one thing, a whiskey bottle just seems to have a peculiar sound of its own.

But still it *could* have been a bottle of liniment or bay rum or who knows what in there. It *could,* I suppose, have been a bottle of ten-dollar perfume that Chic was going to send home to his mother.

And Hammond *could* have simply asked Chic what he had in the bag. If he wanted to be blunt about it, he could've asked Chic if he had any whiskey in camp. I know Chic well enough to know that he'd have owned up to it there and then. He might've been willing to do a lot of things that other people might not, but he wouldn't run and hide from much of anything that he did.

Whatever Hammond could've done, though, what he did do was to give Chic a tight, nasty little grin and then throw the warbag onto the ground at Chic's feet.

There was a sharp, snapping crunch of breaking glass followed by the mellow odor of corn whiskey.

Hammond looked Chic right in the eye and said, "I guess you had something breakable in there, huh? Sorry, kid. You, uh, do know that I don't allow whiskey in this camp."

Now I have given this some thought in the time since then, and I have come to wonder if maybe Hammond wasn't trying to be straight with Chic in his own way, even trying to be nice to him. Hammond was the kind to fire a man if he found him drinking in camp. Maybe this was only his way of getting rid of Chic's bottle without Hammond ever having to see it and acknowledge that it was in his camp. That just could be, though I do not expect to know for sure.

Regardless, right then I was expecting Chic to blow right up, but he did not. He looked at that warbag, wet and leaking through the seams now, and back at Hammond. He bent over and carefully pulled his boots back on, picked up his warbag and laid it aside. He seemed a little more pale than normal — I could not be sure through all that mud — but he was icy calm while he did all this.

When he was quite good and ready he stepped forward, balled his fists and asked, "Ready?"

Hammond was half a head shorter than Chic and twenty years older. He shook his head and said, "You'd be making one hell of a mistake, boy. I didn't set out to fight you."

Chic never answered him and I don't know that he really heard what Hammond said to him.

36

I guess even with all our playing and carrying on I never before had really seen or anyway really appreciated the snake-strike speed Chic Robertson had in his hands. I guess the roping and assorted tomfoolery had never brought it into play before. Certainly not in such a fashion as this.

When Chic moved his right hand it was more like he had pulled a trigger than thrown a punch. One second he was standing there, poised and threatening. The next he was again standing in the exact same way. But in the meantime Chic's balled fist had flashed out to crash with a fearsome speed and power into Hammond's jaw. I heard a loud pop, the way a half-dried limb will sound when it is broken.

Hammond had made no move to defend himself. There was no way he could have. Nothing short of turning and running before Chic decided to swing, there wasn't. I mean, there truly was no way any man could have reacted in time to block it.

That lone punch by Chic was the start, the middle, and the entirety of that whole fight. Once it was thrown Chic was standing there and Willard Hammond was sitting on the ground with his jaw slightly askew. Hammond began to groan.

The foreman stifled the sound he'd started

to make and sat glaring pure venom up at Chic.

"I have some things still in the dugout," Chic said. From the sound of him and from the look of him, he was still as cool and steady as when we had stepped off our horses those few minutes before.

Chic stepped around Hammond, who still hadn't moved, ducked and went into the low shelter. I went to follow.

Hammond held a hand out to stop me. I waited, not really knowing what I could say to the man. He raised one brow over reddened, swelling eyes. It was clear that I was still welcome to stay. But, hell, what could I do? Chic was my partner. And no man could owe another more than I already owed him. I shrugged and stepped around the foreman without trying to explain any of this. I guess he understood it anyhow.

It took only seconds for us to gather our stuff together. Chic glanced once at me and grinned, but he offered no comments. I don't suppose he would've been very surprised that I was coming too.

When we left the dugout Hammond was still by the door but on his feet now. He said nothing, and Chic never once so much as looked his way even though Hammond was wearing a belly gun at the time. I don't believe I could've been that cool about it, but to watch old Chic, there hadn't been anything exciting happen in three weeks or longer. I nodded a silent good-by to Hammond and trailed after Chic.

It was getting pretty dark now away from the cook fire near the dugout, and I stumbled along through the gloom, tripping in the bunches of tough grass and not able to catch up to Chic's dim back without trotting after him like an awkward hound pup, and that I was not willing to do.

The nighthawk had good enough vision to fetch out our personal horses, my bright bay gelding and Chic's handsome yellow horse. Both of them were practically greasy with healthy fat from all the good graze and the light work they'd had lately. The boy riding nightherd delivered them to us and returned to his lonesome work.

We saddled by feel in the darkness and tied our traps in place. I swung into my deep-seated old saddle and sat waiting for Chic to do the same.

After a minute I heard a low whisper from the far side of the yellow horse.

"Bert?"

"Yeah."

"Bert. Help me here a minute, would you?"

"What?"

"Come around here a minute, would you?"

I got off and dropped my reins to ground tie the bay. I walked around to where Chic was standing.

He had hold of the apple of his saddle and was kind of leaning against the leathers, supporting himself there.

"Are you all right, Chic?"

He grinned at me. His teeth and what I could see of his face stood out pale in the dark.

"Look, Bert, would you . . . would you help me up? I guess I'm . . . kinda wobbly in the ol' knees right now."

I touched him on the elbow. He was trembling so hard it was a wonder his teeth weren't rattling.

No one could've been any cooler than he was when he was expecting trouble — and not knowing how far it might go. Now that it was past, he was really shaking. Sheer reaction.

I grabbed him at the waist and between us we got him into the saddle. Once he was up there I knew he'd be all right.

"Bert?" Even his voice was quavery now. "Th-thanks."

"You bet," I told him.

I got back aboard my bay horse and we aimed ourselves more or less northward — mostly, I suppose, because we happened to be on that side of the OX5 dugout and wanted to ride away from it.

"How are we fixed for cash?" I asked Chic the next afternoon. We were hunkered in the shade next to a cool, sweet-tasting little stream there on the north edge of the Strip.

"I got seven dollars left," he said.

"We're in good shape then. I've got three or four left from this pay and a stash tucked away to boot. Eighteen bucks there. Hell, we're the next thing to rich, being the time of month it is."

He flashed that bright, easy grin of his. "You know, we *coulda* been smart enough to bring a little bacon or something with us."

"Not me, man. You can't cook from horseback. I don't think in such lowly terms."

"Tomorra or the next day you'll be thinkin' about it as much as me. Wait an' see if you don't." He lifted his hand out of the running stream and admired the dimples that were where his knuckles used to be.

"Wanta have a roping contest?" I offered. "I'll bet two dollars to your one today."

"You sure aren't much of a gamblin' man,

41

Bert," he said. He looked at the hand again and grimaced. It surely did look bad and must have felt worse. It was puffed and swollen like an inflated bladder. If he didn't have any broken bones under that discolored flesh it was a wonder, for he had really laid one onto Hammond's jaw. They would both be feeling the effects of it for a while. He stuck his hand back into the water. "Do you have any special fancies 'bout where we go from here?"

I shrugged. "There's a lot of places I haven't seen yet. I'm willing to look at any of them at least once."

"Well I've been doin' some thinking about it, 'specially since I won't wanta be usin' a rope again for a little while. I was thinkin' we could go out toward Fort Griffin an' see could we put a stake together shooting buffalo. They say a hide sells for a dollar, an' the critters are supposed to be thick as lice on a squaw out there. Easy money, Bert. Easy money."

I shrugged again, and when we started riding the next time we angled off to the west, toward Chic's visions of easy money.

We stopped at Fort Dodge, which is just east of the cow town where I had been once before. We spent most of our money there. Two dollars each for a pair of Sharps carbines left over from the war. The old loose-powder breech-loaders these were. They had some of those handsome, spanking new .50-90 Sharps rifles, too, with the heavy barrels that you just couldn't hardly shoot out — the kind that was already being called the Old Reliable model — but those were selling for forty-seven dollars each as far east as Kansas. Another eight dollars got us four cases of military-surplus ammunition with the powder and ball ready-loaded in paper cartridges. We also bought a gallon of trade whiskey which we swapped to a greasy-haired Ponca for two ponies to use as pack animals. I think that old Indian got the better of the deal.

Fort Griffin turned out to be a very small amount of something set out in the middle of nothing. A few shacks built of mud and of mud-colored canvas plunked down next to a pair of bare and lonesome ruts. The only thing of any size around the place was the pile of hides stacked along the road. Enough green buffalo hides to make a respectable-sized hill.

"Lordy, Lordy, will you look at all that money," Chic said when he saw that mountain of high-smelling hides. "A dollar of clear profit in each one o' them things, and there must be thousands of 'em there. Tens of thousands. Did I tell you this would be easy money, Bert? Did I?"

"I guess you did, Chic. I sure guess you did."

Chic looked about as eager and as happy as a human could hope to be. His yellow horse, tired as it was, picked up the excitement and began to lift his feet again. Even the Indian ponies quit their stumbling and plodding for a little while there.

We stopped at one of the stores long enough to verify that dollar-a-hide price for buffalo and to invest our last dollar and seventy cents in some dried beans and a bag of salt. Then we declared ourselves in the buffalo-killing business.

I wondered some about the odd little half-smile the store man gave us, but I don't think Chic ever noticed it. But then he was so excited over our prospects I don't believe he'd have noticed if the man had been wearing war paint and a ruffled shirt.

CHAPTER 4

"There's eight of them in there, Chic. We might just as well take them while we have the chance. Eight dollars, Chic. Hell, it's found money, just about."

Chic grunted. He stepped off his yellow horse and hunkered near the edge of the old wash. Down below us in the little brake that had grown up there I'd spotted eight shaggies cooling off in the shade offered by that thin brush.

"I dunno, Bert. Seems to me we oughta go on. Find those mile-wide herds everyone talks about. That's where the easy money is, Bert. Not picking at 'em a few at a time."

I made sure the lead rope of those Indian ponies was securely tied to my saddle horn and then got down to join him. "Look here," I pointed out, "neither of us knows that much about dropping buffs. It wouldn't hurt to get in a little practice before we get into those big herds. Think of it that way.

And we sure could use the meat. I'm getting awful tired of beans."

Chic grinned and gave in. "Get your carbine then, Bert. I guess it won't hurt us none."

I fetched my rust-flecked old carbine from my saddle — at least the old cavalry weapon had a keeper ring on the side, which came in handy for tying the thing to my saddle strings — and got two filled pouches of paper cartridges from the pack on the nearest Indian pony. I gave Chic one of the ammunition pouches and loaded my carbine. It occurred to me that I hadn't thought to fire the thing before, but what the hell. They said buffalo were too stupid to be afraid of gunfire even if you did miss.

We sat with our boots dangling over the edge of that wash and made ourselves comfortable. It was a real lark, some way for a grown man to make a living. I felt like a kid who'd cut himself a fishing pole on his way to school.

The buffalo were maybe seventy-five yards away, dozing as comfortable as could be in the late morning heat. A dry cow switched her ratty tail at the flies and waggled her ears.

"Go ahead, Bert. You're the one that wants 'em. Your shot, pard."

46

I hauled back on that big hammer and set the vee of the sights on the shoulder of the cow. It seemed an easy enough shot.

The trigger pull on that government carbine was something else. More like breaking a twig than easing back on a trigger. It finally let go, and the butt of the stubby carbine walloped my shoulder with a satisfying shove.

"You hit her," Chic said. I couldn't see it myself for all the smoke, a lot more than with a long-barreled rifle. Chic's carbine spouted flame and smoke too.

The buffalo, all eight of them, were in a clumsy gallop up the wash. They passed right by us, not twenty yards away, and both of us sitting there with our carbines empty.

"Who was the idiot who said buffalo don't run from gunfire?"

Chic shrugged. "They are runnin' *toward* it, ain't they?"

A trio of calves were in the lead with the others trailing behind. The old cow was running last and seemed to be faltering. The others scrambled up a loose slide at the far side of the wash. The old cow couldn't make it. She fell back, got to her feet and tried it a second time. Again she fell. She was slower getting to her feet this time. She stood at the bottom of the slide, partially

47

obscured by the dust the others had raised before they disappeared. Her head was hanging.

I slipped another paper cartridge into the breach of the Sharps and seated a musket cap on the big nipple. I touched off the shot.

"You're low," Chic said. "That one raised dirt under her belly." The smoke cleared, and he fired. A moment later I saw a splash of dust on the cow's flank. She twitched a little and began to turn in ponderous circles. I reloaded and fired again. After a while the cow sank onto her knees and rolled over.

"How 'bout that," Chic said. "One silver dollar, right there for the taking."

"It sounds too easy to be true," I said.

And I was right.

It was maybe four hundred yards up to where the cow had dropped, and because of the steep sides of the wash we had to slither down the bank and walk to her, leaving the horses where they stood. And believe me it was plenty hot walking down in there for no wind — of which there wasn't hardly any to start with — could reach down there below ground level. We both were sopping wet before we ever reached the carcass.

The cow was something of a mess. The hide dirty and her sides matted with blood. A swarm of bluebottle flies had already found their treat.

"I'll tell you somethin', Bert. I never beefed one of these things before. How do you go about butcherin' one?"

"Now I will be double-damned, Chic Robertson. I thought *you* were the expert here."

He just grinned at me.

For a few minutes there we just stood and admired that dead cow. Then Chic began shuffling around, looking at her from this angle and then from that. When he got tired of that, he pulled his belt knife and admired it for a time.

I had a heavy folding knife that I'd always thought pretty highly of, but when I unlimbered it now it seemed just the least bit puny for the task. Regardless, it had to be done. We both set in to slicing and hacking at about the same time.

Now I will give you a word of advice. Don't ever — never — let any fool tell you that it is an easy thing to yank the hide from a dead buffalo. No, indeed.

I have pulled the hides from a fair number of winter-killed beeves, but this chore was nowhere near in the same class as that. Maybe it has something to do with the weather or with those winter die-up carcasses having time to cure or something. Or maybe it is just the difference in the two kinds of animals. I surely wouldn't know. Whatever, the difference is considerable.

The two of us sliced and tugged and rassled ourselves all over and around that cow, and before long you'd have thought we just stepped out of a warm tub of sweat and congealing blood. Lordy, but it was a mess.

The thing is, you can't just grab hold of a buffalo hide and peel it back the way you can with a beef. Both the hair and the skin seem ten times thicker than on a beef. So one of us would grab and pull while the other reached under to slice away the tissues that were trying to defeat us. Once in a while, too, one of us would make a slip and cut the hide instead of those tissues.

Still, we kept after it, and eventually we had the hide off. Most of it, anyway.

"Chic, do you get the impression that maybe there's a trick to this that we haven't learned yet?"

"Uh huh." He slumped down next to the gouged and liberally sliced naked carcass. He started to wipe the sweat off his forehead but took a look at the gore on his hands and arms and decided otherwise. "Sheesh!"

"If someone offered me a dollar to do that again right now, I'd spit in his eye."

"I wouldn't," Chic said. "I'd go straight to

shooting an' leave out all that other fuss."

It would've been nice to just sit and cool off for a few minutes, but there was no cooling off going to be done down there in that airless furnace, and the flies were bother enough to send Job round the bend. "Let's get out of here," I suggested.

Chic nodded. He looked too weary to reply in words.

We discovered then that a buffalo hide is one heavy damned thing. Call it forty pounds of pure awkward. There's no handle on one to carry it by, and they stink, and the flies tend to follow wherever the hide leads. Each of us packed the thing halfway back to the horses, and we made the scramble back up the dropoff, Chic with our precious buffalo hide and me clattering the two carbines together.

Chic draped the hide over one of the ponies and pulled his sweat-plastered shirt away from his ribs. "Do you know what we went an' did?" he asked.

"I'd believe almost anything."

"We walked off an' forgot to bring any meat off that thing."

I shook my head. That was near about the last straw for the day. "Isn't it a good thing that I love beans?"

"Ain't it, though," he agreed. It was for

51

sure that neither one of us wanted a half-mile hike there and back for a piece of sun-baked, fly-blown meat. Old Chic looked at me and I stared back at him, and directly he began to snicker. Pretty soon the both of us were howling-out-loud laughing. Which I suppose is a lot better than weeping.

A dozen miles further on we found a slime-scummed pothole that used to be a pond and likely would be again when the rains came — assuming they ever did in this part of the country. Whatever, there was enough water hidden under the surface trash for us to let the horses take as much as they wanted. And it didn't taste half as bad as it looked if you boiled beans in it long enough.

We got ourselves more or less cleaned up and decided to stay right there on the theory that buffalo would be coming by for a drink evening and morning, and it would be easier for them to find us than for us to go looking for them. Like with so many theories, that one was a fine idea but worked a little less well when put into practice. What happened was that we had a nice, quiet evening.

In the morning there still weren't any shaggies beating their heads against our carbines trying to get to the water, but a couple hours after sunup a short train of four wagons rolled into view over a rise so low I hadn't even known it was there. They were within a half mile of us before we saw them.

Like I said, there were the four wagons, each of them great heavy things with extra wide iron tires gleaming in the slanting sunshine. Each wagon was pulled by a six-mule hitch and had both a driver and a helper on the box. There were also two men on horses plodding along close to the wagons. When they got a little closer we could see that one wagon held a jumble of boxes, crates, and stuff, but the others seemed to be empty. They were pretty obviously heading for our water hole. When they were within a few hundred yards the outriders touched up their horses and came ahead.

We stood and fingered our hatbrims, and the two men stepped down without waiting for an invitation. Of course we *were* at a watering place, and maybe they figured that gave them the right.

Both of them were hard-looking characters with untrimmed beards and heavy jackboots, and both were hung pretty heavily with knives and pistols.

"Mornin'," I said. Chic for some reason was hanging back this morning.

"Ayup," the taller, darker of the two

grunted. He looked at our stuff strewn on the ground and said, "You boys are a fair piece away from cow country. Unless some fool drover is thinking about bringing beef up here . . . ?" He let that hang in the air for a while.

"Not that we'd know of," I told him. "We came out thinking we'd shoot a buffalo or two for a change of pace."

"Uh huh," the man said. He seemed to relax a little.

They introduced themselves as Iver Cord and Lester Hanks, Cord being the taller one who'd spoken first.

"You boys ever seen the big buff'lo herds?" Hanks asked.

"Not yet," I told him.

"That's something of a shame, 'cause now you never will. They're all thinned down and scattered now. Broken up for good and all. They'll never be back."

His partner, Cord, gave him a hard look. "I told you before to quit talkin' like that, Lester. Couple mild winters and there'll be as many of 'em as ever there was. And I don't wanta hear you saying otherwise."

Hanks grinned. He hooked a thumb toward Cord. "Iver an' me have been arguing about that for the past two year, ever since we got into the business. He claims it'll go on forever. I say we should make our pile an' save out enough to get us started in another line of work one of these days."

"That's what you do for a living then? Shoot buffs?" It was the first thing Chic had bothered to say.

"You damn well betcha," Hanks said. "Me'n Iver took eleven thousand four hundred and sixty two hides last year, an' that ain't bad." He seemed awfully proud of that, and well he might. That came to an awful lot of money, near six thousand apiece. And a top foreman with a good cow outfit probably wouldn't make more than nine hundred, most likely closer to six hundred. And a waddie? Why, he'd be lucky if he pulled in three hundred in a year's time. Chic whistled right out loud when he heard that, and I guess I showed what I was thinking too. Hanks laughed and slapped his partner across the shoulders. "You can see why Iver wants to think it'll never stop."

The wagons rumbled up to us with an empty bounce and clatter. Eleven thousand hides. No wonder these boys wanted big wagons with wide, go-anywhere tires on them. The drivers and helpers — at close range we could see they were mostly Mexicans — got a nod from Cord and began breaking the hitches long enough to water the mules and then hook them back into the chains. They did it quickly, with a good bit of laughing and carrying on.

"You boys say you're looking to shoot a few buff'lo yourselves," Hanks said. I nodded at him. "Well, you won't see but a handful of stragglers around here right now. Tell you what," he said. He gave our outfit another glance, and I guess it did look sorta pitiful to his eyes. "Tell you what now. You aren't going to run me'n Iver out of business with your competition. Why don't you ride along and we'll show you how it's done. We'll reach what's left of the southern herd in another three or four days. You can't do any worse than waste that much time."

I looked at Chic, and he jerked his chin for me to follow him away a little piece. "I'll let you know in a minute," I told Hanks and followed Chic. "What in the world do you want to talk it over for?" I asked when we were out of earshot.

It sounded like an awful good idea to me. I mean, what could we possibly lose by it? These men knew the business of turning buffalo into lap robes and harness leather and what-have-you. And since they made the offer — free for nothing — to show us how they did it, it seemed we'd be foolish to turn them down. Which is just what I told Chic I thought about it.

"Bert, I just don't know," Chic said, shaking his head. He was examining the toes of his boots but soon he looked up at me. "I got a feeling in me that says we oughta stay clear of these boys. No, that ain't exactly right either. Of Cord. That Hanks seems like an all right sort. But there's somethin' about that other fella that doesn't set quite right with me. You know what I mean?"

"No, I don't guess I do, but it's all right with me, Chic. If you wanta stay clear, then we will. I'll just tell Hanks we appreciate it, but we'll pass." I went to turn away, but Chic caught me by the sleeve. When I looked back at him he had that open, easy grin of his on him.

"Aw, hell, Bert. Nev' mind. I'm just bein' silly about this. An' you're right. It's a good chance for us to learn about downin' buffs." His grin got wider. "Easy money, Bert. That's what it's gonna be. Eleven thousand those fellas made last year? Hell, Bert, tell 'em we'll come along."

"Only if you're sure you want to."

He nodded. "Sure I'm sure. We cain't pass up a chance like that. Tell 'em we're comin'."

CHAPTER 5

They found the scattered southern herd on the fourth day, just like Hanks had predicted, which only goes to show how well these boys knew their business. And let me tell you, Hanks and Cord might have been disappointed that the herd didn't spread in a solid brown blanket from horizon to horizon, but personally I would not have thought there could be so many animals in all of Texas much less that you could see so many of one kind with a single sweep of your eyes.

Sure they were broken up into bands of them. But some of those bands must have held a thousand animals. And everywhere you looked there were more and more and yet more black-brown splotches of buffalo. I believe you could have ridden for hour after hour and maybe day after day without ever once managing to be as much as a half mile from one or more of those bands of slow-moving buffalo.

I've seen cattle going up the trail during the peak of the drover days, and at first some of those old boys ran as many as five thousand head in a single trail herd. I've seen the times and the places where one of those trail herds wouldn't be out of sight before another was in view coming up from the south. But I never before and never since saw so many four-legged creatures as there were buffalo on that grass south and east of Fort Griffin. And no matter that they say the day of the buffalo was already past then, I'm glad I got to see as much of it as I did.

We set up our camp right in the thick of them, a dozen miles from the nearest water. What the buffalo did for water — if there were so many that we never noticed them shifting to and from water or if they got all the moisture they needed from the short grass — I never did figure out. What Hanks and Cord did was to send the one supply wagon each and every day to haul barrels of fresh water for the men and mules and horses in the outfit.

It pretty soon became apparent too that those drivers and helpers on the other wagons were not along for the purpose of holding the wagon seats in place.

Come the first morning of the hunt, Cord led off with one empty wagon in one direction while Hanks rode another direction with another wagon. We trailed along with Hanks since Chic had taken such a dislike to Cord that they still weren't more than grunting at each other when conversation seemed necessary. And that was not frequent.

Hanks spent better than an hour nosing around here and there between the bands — the wagon lumbering along a half mile or so behind — until he found a setup to his liking.

"I'll mark my stand right over there," he explained with a gesture. There was maybe the tiniest hint of elevation where he was pointing, and beyond it was a band of maybe three hundred buffalo. "The wind's coming toward us, you see, and they're grazing crossways to it. Just right for what I want."

He took his own sweet time about getting a picket pin from his saddle pockets and driving the pin into the ground. He tied his horse there and checked each knot twice before he was satisfied. From the other pocket he took a bulging sack of ammunition.

His rifle he carried in a hard-backed case

that he'd had strapped under his leg. Now he opened the case in much the same way a good fiddler will uncase his violin when he gets to the site of a big dance on a Saturday night. The weapon was a pretty one sure enough and probably worth all that fuss.

It was a Sharps, which I'd expected, but I'd never seen one as fine as this. It was no longer than your store-rack Sharps, but the barrel was about as thick as a man's wrist. The heavy-barreled store Sharps will weigh out at fourteen pounds or so. This would've been more like twenty pounds or greater. The barrel was octagon shape, blued not browned, and burnished to a gloss that would've put most jewels to shame.

The wood was even nicer. Fancy grained walnut with the veining of the grain swooping and swirling through and around but always in harmony with the shape of the stock. Just by looking at it you knew someone had spent days searching for just the right blank of stump-cut wood before he ever thought of making that first, small chisel cut to commence his artistry. And polished? The blued metal looked positively dull in comparison. That part too would've taken a patient man half of forever to get to such a condition.

On the whole of the rifle there was not

the first line of checkering nor the first scratch of engraving to detract from the beauty that someone had put into wood and steel. No gimcracks or geegaws here, for such work could only have cheapened what Hanks had here.

It fired — and I know because I asked — a .50-110 cartridge. A .50-caliber, 520-grain bullet in front of a hundred ten grains of imported powder.

The sights were contained in a full-barrel-length steel tube wedded securely to the barrel. It was a kind of rig I'd not seen before.

Hanks was pleased by the admiration his rifle drew from both of us. He seemed tickled to talk about it, how it'd been made up for him on special order at a cost of three hundred fifty dollars plus freight and packing. But he sure never offered to hand it around to us, and I do not blame him for that.

He looked it over and felt of it for a minute and then took from another compartment of the case a collapsible, three-legged rest with a sheepskin-padded notch for the barrel to lie in. This he let me carry as we approached the shooting stand.

I was a little surprised, but he made no effort to hide himself from the buffalo he was about to shoot. We just walked over there and watched while Hanks made himself comfortable.

He took the tripod and positioned it just so and sat cross-legged behind it. The ammunition sack he laid out at just the comfortable distance from his knee so that his hand fell naturally to it. Finally he hefted the big Sharps into place, checked the bore for obstructions, and slid a cartridge into the chamber. I figured it was damn well about time.

The wagon, meanwhile, had stopped about a quarter mile back. The Mexican crew was having themselves a smoke. I could see them sprawled in the shade of the wagon box.

The big rifle spoke, and I looked around. I guess I expected to see the band of buffalo tail-flagging it at a high run like so many spooked steers and to hear a string of fast shots. Instead nothing much of interest seemed to be happening. Hanks was taking his time about extracting his empty shell, replacing it in the sack and loading a fresh one into the rifle. He even paused to examine the bullet in the fresh cartridge before he decided to use it.

I leaned closer to Chic and whispered, "What happened? Did he miss?"

"Not hardly." Chic pointed off to the left. A couple hundred yards away a buff at the edge of the herd had sunk to its knees. While I was watching, it quietly, slowly rolled onto its side. The other animals in the vicinity paid no attention. They were grazing as calmly as if they hadn't heard the shot, although they absolutely must have.

Hanks picked out another, again on the fringe of the band, and carefully squeezed off his shot. I was watching the animal this time and caught the dust puff of bullet impact behind the shoulder. It was a bit higher and further back than I would've expected. The buffalo, a cow it was, flinched a little and tossed its head, but it didn't bolt. It stood there and shortly began to wobble. Pretty soon it was on the ground.

Hanks still was in no hurry about anything. He just patiently went about his business, dropped ten of them before he took a break to smoke and let the Sharps barrel cool. He was on his sixteenth before he muffed one. The bullet hit on the shoulder itself. The bull half fell, righted itself, and let out a bellow. Within seconds the entire band was at a run.

"Damn!" Hanks muttered. Now his fingers were flying as they plucked out the spent cartridge and rammed in a fresh one.

Hanks came to his feet, threw all that rifle weight to his shoulder and made a really pretty running shot as the wounded bull quartered away from him.

The bull skidded into a lump, and the rest of the band raced away through an open avenue between two other, still completely undisturbed bands. Hanks waved his arms, and the two Mexicans began bringing the wagon up.

Hanks gathered his things together, sacked up his ammunition and empties, folded his tripod, and gently latched the rifle away into its case after taking the time to run a few wet patches through the bore.

The Mexicans paid no attention to their boss. They knew their business and set about it while Hanks went on with his.

They drove the wagon to the nearest of the dead buffalo and dropped the pair of lead mules out of the hitch. One of the men made a few quick incisions along the belly and legs of the buff while the other man rigged some chain tugs to the free team of mules.

Stout hooks at the ends of those chains were punched through folds of skin at the rear end of the buffalo. A twitch on the driving lines and those mules peeled the hide off as easy as a man would skin a rabbit.

One Mexican handled the mules while the other man stood over the carcass with his knife blade flashing, slicing neatly through the tough connecting tissues whenever they threatened to hang or tear. It was a slick, quick operation. Within a couple minutes the hide was off, folded and in the wagon, and they were driving the wagon and the loose team to the next carcass.

"You don't take any of the meat?" I asked Hanks. He had finished his repacking chores and was taking time for a smoke.

"Naw," he said. "Not worth the trouble. There's some that save the tongues. Pack them in brine and sell them back east. But hell, when you figure the cost of your barrels and the salt and haulage, it ain't worth the few cents you can make on it."

"Not even for your own use you don't save any?"

"Oh, they'll fetch back a couple humps to use tonight." He grinned. "That's one good thing about a buffalo camp. A man can't hardly go hungry."

Chic shook his head. I guess like me he was thinking how slick and easy these boys made it look. And so much meat they could just leave it lay there to rot, whatever of it wasn't eaten by the buzzards and the wolves and all the other scavengers that followed the buffalo herds and the hide wagons.

Coming from country full of cheap cattle — and a good many of them unbranded and free for the taking back when I was a kid — I'd never known what it was to go hungry. But a lot of the men who'd come back from the war still talked in tones of shock and pity about the hunger they'd seen back east. For that matter, it was simple meat-hunger in the east that turned the wheels and made the fortunes in the cow business. A range cow still wasn't worth a damn except as a walking commissary. I had to wonder what those people would've thought — those people who had to depend on someone else to supply their meat a pound at a time at ten cents or even more — if they could've seen all that rich red meat lying there in the sun. It made me sorta think.

Hanks gave us a come-along sign and got onto his horse. He didn't bother to wait for his skinning crew but headed straightaway to choose his next shooting stand. The wagon would follow when they were ready, which would not be long as quick as those boys worked.

They went easily, almost casually through the day like that with each stand producing its greater or lesser addition to the load on the big wagon. At one place Hanks dropped only two cows before something — not his shooting — spooked the band and sent them running. He was some kind of mad about that. When he decided in his own leisurely way to knock off for the day, he had fifty-three buffs on the ground, and it was still fairly early in the day. There was a reason even for that.

"The crew needs time to stake these hides and flesh them," Hanks explained. "The buyers want clean, dry, flint hides. Or the buggers dock you for the damage. Can't hardly make any money that way."

"Can we watch how they do it?" Chic asked. He'd been interested the whole day long but not especially cheerful.

"Sure," Hanks said, "but it's dull stuff, I warn you. Not the kind of thing a white man wants to do." He shrugged his shoulders. "But suit yourself. Let's find a cup of coffee until the wagon comes in."

CHAPTER 6

We gave it the good old try those next few days, and it was for sure there were enough buffalo around for us to try our skills at. We stayed on with the Hanks and Cord outfit but made it a point to go off in directions that would not interfere with their work. After all, they were being awfully nice about letting us share their camp and their coffee, even Cord who would've really preferred for us to be somewhere else.

It didn't take long to discover that, with our beat-up old military carbines, our best bet was for us to work together, shooting together at one animal and hoping to get a clean drop on that one without disturbing the rest. Once in a while we could do it, but for the most part we would get one and spook the rest. As a result we took to picking the smallest bands we could find so we would cause the least disturbance in the herd. We didn't want to mess things up for

Hanks or for the other shooting crews —
and there were a surprising number of them
— working in and around the huge southern
herd.

Dropping a buffalo wasn't the problem,
though, nor was skinning them once we
learned the trick of it. We got so we could
peel the hides fairly slick by using one of
our saddle horses to supply the power and a
plain old *reata* to hook on with. Nossir, the
problem was in fleshing those damn hides.

Just like Hanks had told us, the hides had
to be tended properly if they were going to
dry cleanly. The message was reinforced
when we discovered that that first hide we'd
taken was spoiled already. Patches of rot
were well started in the folds and wherever
bits of tissue had been allowed to remain
on the hide. We'd done all that work and all
that sweating for absolutely nothing. We had
to throw the hide away, a dead loss.

And fleshing a hide . . . sheesh! Hands-
and-knees work with a bone scraper in the
full heat of the sun, hour after hour of that
with your back a pulp of shooting pains
until when you finally did stand up you were
still bent half-doubled with tightened
muscles and fresh cramps. It didn't help
either that we were not exactly adept at this
kind of work and it took us three or maybe

even four times as long to work over a fresh hide.

Once they were scraped, the hides were allowed to dry flint hard while they were staked flat on the ground — with borrowed pegs since we had none of our own and there was no wood around for cutting fresh ones.

After four days of miserably hard work we had exactly nineteen hides in our little pile. And old Chic was looking about as miserable as the work had been. After supper that night — buffalo hump broiled over a buffalo-chip fire, followed by buffalo marrow for a dessert of sorts — Chic slumped down beside the feeble, almost invisible flames with a weary sigh.

"Bert," he said, "we got a problem."

"I got an achin' back and a sunburnt neck. What else do you figure I got?"

"Bert, this buff'lo hunting ain't exactly easy money is what I'm thinking."

I couldn't help but grin at the woebegone look my usually cheerful partner was wearing. "I will not argue with you," I told him. I guess his back was as wire-bound stiff as mine felt just then.

Chic leaned back cautiously until he was propped on one elbow. He sighed. "I don't even know if we're gonna get *any*thing out o' this, Bert."

I gave him a questioning look and glanced around toward our carefully scraped and dried and stacked little pile of green hides. It was an indistinct lump in the darkness beyond that day's take of three hides now pegged out flat on the ground. "What's the matter with them? They're all right, aren't they? Worth a few bucks, just like we expected?"

"Sure," Chic grumped at me. "But look at the damn things, Bert. Just look at 'em." He pointed toward them with his chin. His expression was pretty sour. "Each one of 'em laid flat an' half a mile wide. An' they gotta stay that way, Bert. They gotta be carried flat, the same way as they dried. You ever think o' that?"

I shook my head. I really hadn't thought of it, either.

"Well I did. This afternoon when we was layin' those new ones onto the pile. Those things've got no more bend in 'em than a pine sapling. Just so much an' then they start t' crack. They'll not be worth more than fifty cents or so. I asked. An', Bert, you 'n me got no way to haul those things flat. Not on pack horses, we don't."

Great. That meant we had only half as much as we thought. No wonder Chic was looking so glum. "We did better than this nursemaiding other folks' cows," I said. "I don't suppose . . . ?" I let it tail off with a sort of half-hopeful lift at the end.

"I don't know, Bert. I sure as hell don't." Ol' Chic surely did sound just then like a *de*jected, *re*jected, *un*happy man. Things just weren't working out the way he'd expected them to. I guess he'd really had visions of cartwheel dollars falling by the bagful into our laps as soon as we waved our carbine muzzles in the direction of a buffalo herd. It seemed to upset him to find he'd been wrong. That this buffalo hunting was a business that took some investment in wagons and draft animals and supplies and, mostly, in hired help if it was going to pay out.

Me, I didn't care so much as all that. We had work to do during the day and plenty of food to eat when the working was done. And if the pay turned out to be less than we'd figured, well, we'd just raise a little less hell after we sold our hides.

"I'm thinkin' maybe we should try something else, Bert," Chic said after a little silence. "Would you mind?"

"Mind? Would I *mind* being able to sit on a horse again instead of crawling around with a scraper in my hand and a crick in my

73

back? Would I *mind* lying down at night without some fool sneaking up behind to jab me with a red-hot poker every time I move? Would I *mind* that, Chic? Well I guess I would not mind it overmuch, now that you suggest it."

"Yeah," Chic said. He was grinning again.

And just like that Chic was back to being his normal self. Once the decision was made to forget this foolishness, he seemed to figure it was already over and done with and could be put behind him as an incident of the past. He took out his knife and sliced a generous chunk off the buffalo hump we'd been eating for dinner. He poked a wiping rod through the slab of meat and dangled it over the fire, though it hadn't been a half hour since we'd finished eating. "Better have some more o' this," he said cheerfully. "We ain't gonna have a chance at it much longer."

That seemed kind of silly, so soon after a big meal, but that strip of fresh meat did look and smell pretty good hanging over that fire with the rich juices just bubbling out of it. So I did join him, and the two of us sat there in the middle of all those buffalo and gorged ourselves until we were stuffed like a pair of toads. Damned if it wasn't fun, too.

■ ■ ■ ■

"Where's Hanks?" Chic asked. He sounded as if the words tasted bad in his mouth, having to speak them to Iver Cord. Whatever it was between those two — and I couldn't see any call for there to be anything wrong there — the two of them were like flint and steel every time they came together.

"Huntin'," Cord said shortly.

"We wanted to talk to 'im about a business matter," Chic said. I could tell plain enough that he was having to force himself to be civil to the man. In truth, of course, Cord had been every bit as generous to us as Hanks because it was just as much his water and his coffee we'd been sharing as they were Hanks'.

Cord screwed his face into knots, first to one side and then to the other. He worked up a cheekful of spit and let fly. It wasn't anywhere near Chic nor his boots, but Chic began to look like there was an ice-laden norther blowing around inside him. "If it's business I reckon I can handle it as good as Lester," Cord said.

Chic grunted once, and I took a step nearer. What I was thinking was that with Hanks gone maybe I should do the talking, even though this was another of Chic's ideas we had come to discuss. He looked at me and seemed to know what I was thinking. He gave me a tiny headshake to wave me off.

"Look here, Cord," he said with a sharp edge in his tone, "you people know this hunting business, but it ain't for us. We see that clear now an' we figure to get out of it."

Cord nodded as if to say that he agreed we had no business messing into something we knew nothing about. And I don't think that set too well with Chic either.

Chic swallowed hard once but went on. "You know we can't haul our hides back to Fort Griffin without damaging them, cuttin' their value in half, right?" Again Cord nodded. "So what I thought," Chic said, "was maybe we could cut our loss in half, see, an' give you fellows a little profit out o' that loss, you see?"

Iver Cord pondered the idea slowly, turning it over and examining it from all sides to judge from the faces he was making. He got a kind of smug look about him and said, "Sixty cents. Take it or leave it." So yeah, he knew what Chic'd been talking about all right.

I got to give Chic credit for keeping hold

of himself since he'd started it. "What I had in mind," he said in a slow, dead level drawl, "was an even split of the difference. You can have our hides for seventy-five cents as bein' fair to the both of us."

"Take it or leave it was what I told you."

An icy little piece of a smile tugged at Chic's mouth. "Generous son of a bitch, ain't you?"

Cord's hostility, so near the surface anyway, burst into the open now. His face flushed near purple with anger. He stood eyeball to eyeball with Chic and glared at him. The both of them were tall, well setup men but Cord was the older and heavier built and looked by far the meaner of the pair. "You low, cow-punching scum, you. Too damned miserable for honest work. Soon as you might have to turn a lick of it, you come begging to your betters for them to do everything for you. Well, don't expect me to powder your bottom or change your didies, cowpuncher. I got no use for the likes of you."

Chic smiled, but there was sure no hint of gaiety in it. "Maybe less generous an' more son of a bitch than I first figured," he said straight to the man's face.

With a squawl of quick rage, Iver Cord exploded. His right boot smashed into

Chic's knee, and he dragged a long, heavy-bladed knife from its scabbard at his belt.

The kick had landed hard, and Chic was already hurting. He caught his balance just as Cord's knife slashed in a wicked, sweeping arc toward his belly. Chic fell back, barely in time to slide out of reach of the knife's edge.

With a grunt of effort, Cord ripped the big knife down and back across for another pass as he moved closer. Chic was stumbling backward now, intent on trying to get away.

It had happened so quick that at first I was just standing there like an uninterested spectator or something, but I finally did get my wits together a little and moved toward them.

Cord slashed again and while it did not seem to reach the body — Cord was between me and Chic now and I could not see too well — there was a spattering of bright red on the ground.

I did the only thing I could think of with no gun close to hand. I raised up and kicked Iver Cord as hard as I could low in the back, just about at the base of his backbone.

That seemed to get his attention. The shock of it emptied the air from Cord's lungs with an explosive "uhff." He went down to his knees and on backward until he was seated on the ground like a kid playing in a mud puddle. He seemed for the moment to have forgotten about that heavy, half-red knife of his, so I took advantage of his lapse to reach around from behind and pluck the thing out of his fingers.

It was a weighty damn thing, about as much as a hatchet and twice as vicious. Good for chopping wood or slicing throats, either one. I threw it well out of reach, and the big blade spun through the sunlight with bright, gleaming flashes of polished metal.

"You might've busted my back, Fella," Cord said. He sounded calm enough. There was a hint of complaint in his voice but no real anger.

"Well, I didn't go to do that anyway," I told him. Cord lay back on the hard ground and seemed to turn his attention inward while he was deciding if he was bad hurt or not.

Chic was hunkered down a few feet beyond with his hands clamped together. They were both pretty gory and at first it looked like he'd tried to ward off a swipe of the blade with his hands. I knelt beside him and pried his hands apart. A closer look showed that only one of them was contributing to the mess. There was a deep gash on the edge of his left hand between the thumb and the wrist. It was bleeding pretty vigorously but seemed to be a clean enough slice that would take a bandage without too much fuss.

I turned to Cord and asked him, "I don't suppose you have a clean cloth on you?" He reached into a coat pocket and pulled out a mostly clean linen handkerchief. "Thanks," I told him.

Cord let his head fall back into the grass and concentrated on moving his feet, one at a time rotating them at the ankle. From the faraway look on him, I would say he was still wondering if they were going to work each time he told them to. I can't really blame him. I guess we've all seen men who've come off a horse wrong and landed on their back and never taken another step again. That is reason enough for worry.

I didn't make any attempt to wipe the sticky blood off Chic's hand but folded the handkerchief and tied it tightly in place to close the wound so it could quit bleeding and start healing.

"That hurts," Chic said when I pulled the first knot snug.

"It hasn't hardly started to," I said and tugged it once more before I tied it off.

"You got no sympathy in you at all, do you, Bert?"

"Nope. I know damn good and well you're gonna use this as an excuse to make me do all the camp work now."

He grinned. "I'd already thought o' that."

"I figured you would."

"You boys aren't going to come down on Lester about this, are you?" Cord asked. I had almost forgotten the man until he spoke again.

"I don't see why we should," I told him. "He's always been strictly white with us."

"Good," Cord said. He sounded genuinely relieved. "He gets pretty upset with me sometimes."

"I ain't mad at him about anything," Chic said. The bandage was already spotted through, but you could tell it wasn't spreading so fast now.

Cord lay there for a while chewing on some stray beard hairs that were straggling into the corners of his mouth. "Help me up, will you, Fella?" he asked after a minute or so.

I helped him to his feet, though he wasn't having any trouble with his legs that I could see. Chic stood too and carefully wiped his right hand on his pants leg. Chic still had a small knife at his belt while Cord's was well out of reach. If Cord was aware of how close Chic's hand was to that knife handle, he gave no sign of it.

"Look here, boys," Cord mumbled, "you promised me you wouldn't say anything to Lester, right?"

"I guess so," I said. Chic just shrugged.

Cord pulled a bull-scrotum purse — buffalo I would guess — from his pocket and dipped two fingers into it. He took a coin from it and pressed the shiny yellow disc into my hand. It was a double eagle. "That should cover the value of your hides," he said. "You don't hafta bring Lester into this at all."

"You don't even know how many hides you're buying," I protested. I mean, hell, that was a dollar more than we could've gotten for them at Fort Griffin.

"I got a close enough idea," Cord said with a shift of his eyes toward the Mexican wagon crews still waiting and watching from a safe distance. "Is it a deal?"

"You just bought some hides," I said quickly, before Chic would have a chance to open his mouth. Neither of us offered to shake on the deal.

Chic and I got onto our horses and stopped just long enough for me to throw our gear onto the pack animals. We were a couple miles on our way before Chic got around to asking me how much Cord had paid for our hides. He grinned when I told him, but I noticed that he didn't say anything about it being easy money. But then I imagine that by that time his hand was throbbing pretty good with every step that yellow horse took.

CHAPTER 7

We went north again for no especially good reason and two days later found a trio of fuzz-bearded kids lolling around in a plum brake along the Canadian. They invited us to stay the night and as they had nearly a full bag of ground coffee we agreed.

They none of them looked to be more than seventeen; kids running off from the farm in search of something they hoped would be more exciting. They said they were from Bremer County, Iowa, and sounded so proud of it that I was tempted to ask them why they'd run from it. But of course I did not. And they did genuinely seem like nice boys.

"Are you fellas really cowpunchers?" the kid named Harvey Griffith asked when our horses were tended and we'd settled by their fire. Harvey was the least of the litter for size, but that didn't seem to bother him any. He was dark haired and deep tanned and as quick as a bird in his movements and speech. You got the idea that he never could have made a farmer, for he wouldn't have been able to abide the pace of walking behind a plow.

Chic made a fierce face and leaped to his feet, his hand going to his knife. "You tryin' to insult us, farm boy?" he demanded.

Harvey seemed considerable surprised, but I noticed that his chin shot up and out. He wasn't backing off any, though I don't think there was any way he could have known that Chic was funning him.

Chic looked my way and growled, "A dollar says I can take his ear off without scratchin' his cheek."

"Aw, these boys are just ignorant, Chic. The Christian thing would be to give them a chance to learn." I winked at Harvey and added, "But if they don't, you can lop *both* his ears off."

Chic laughed and sat back down. He curled his hands around his coffee cup, the rusty-colored bandage showing spots of white in the last of the daylight.

Tommy Mabry and Julius Raskin, the other farm boys, looked like they still half believed it, but Harvey hadn't turned a hair the whole time. "What's so insulting about that, anyhow? You fellas got something

85

against cowpunchers?"

Chic leaned forward and thumped him on the breastbone with a stiffened forefinger. "Don't you go callin' a cowhand no puncher, boy. Say it t' the wrong one an' you might get yourself stomped down, cut up, an' shot full o' holes, all at the same time."

"Cowpunchers," I told him, "are a bunch of bums. Railroaders and drunks and other such riffraff. They ride the cattle cars with poles to prod the steers up if they should go down in the cars, see, and they don't need any more sense than knowing how to poke something with a stick and maybe pick the lice and the coal cinders outta their hair. A cow*hand,* now, has to know something about the bovine mind and be man enough to do a job of work."

Harvey nodded just as serious as could be and said, "I think I see the difference now. Anybody could be a cowpuncher, but it takes a man with the brains of a cow to make a hand. Uh huh."

Old Chic reared back and let out a roar of laughter. "B'God, Harvey, you figured it out all right. Bert, which one of us is more cowbrained than the other?"

"I wouldn't rightly know," I told him, "unless you count that I can rope better than you. That must mean *some*thing."

He grinned again. "A dollar says you cain't. Wait'll I get this rag off my hand an' I'll show you which one's the better."

We sipped our coffee and ate some of the boys' bacon, which we hadn't tasted for quite a while and so went down awfully nice again for a change.

Chic was munching the last of his bacon when he got sort of a faraway, speculative kind of look in his eyes for a moment. He swallowed and mused out loud, "Sure cain't compare that to buff'lo meat." He made a big show of bringing his attention back to the boys and in a louder voice said, "Say now, I sure didn't mean t' be ungrateful t' you boys. Nossir, I didn't. You all've been mighty generous an' friendly, an' that's a fact. It's just that once you've had buff'lo meat out there in the Big Hunt, why, there just ain't anything else can compare."

Now me, I was a little curious about Chic's sense of taste and good judgment when he said a thing like that. I will admit that buffalo is about as good a meat as can be found, but a man would get tired of champagne and oysters if that's all he had to eat day in and day out for a long enough time, and Chic'd been eating nothing but buffalo every bit as long as I had.

He sure got the attention of those boys, though. You could practically see their ears perking up and growing pointy with their interest. A body would think the word "buffalo" was something magical.

"We've never seen a real buffalo," Harvey said.

"Just hides," Julius said. "Hundreds and hundreds of them on the rail cars. You wouldn't think there could be that much of anything."

Chic leaned back and smiled tolerantly down from the height of superior knowledge. "Boys," he said, "you just ain't seen nothing 'til you've seen the southern herd. Bert an' me just come from there, two days south, an' let me tell you, it is *some*. There's so many critters I swear a man could ride for a month an' wear out ten horses an' never ride his way around that whole herd. More'n a body could ever imagine. Easy t' shoot, too, an' the hides worth a yankee dollar for each one. An' eager buyers?" He rolled his eyes. "Me 'n Bert sold our hides out there in the herd without even havin' t' haul them to a market."

Chic shook his head and gave me a baleful look. "Ol' Bert's just set on runnin' cows for a livin' or we'd be there yet, boys. But he's made up his mind an' we're partners, so here we be, by damn. Much of a waste as I think it is, here we be."

"We could always go back if you feel so strong about it," I told him.

He waved a hand with a great show of patience and understanding. "No," he said, "we talked it out an' made our decision. We can just stick to it now. It means more t' you than it does t' me, an' that's a fact. An' I ain't complainin', Bert. You know that. I jus' think it's a damn shame t' let a pair o' good Sharps buff'lo guns an' a pair of Indian-trained buff'lo ponies go t' such waste. Got no use for such stuff workin' cows, an' you know it. I just hate t' see all that investment go to waste, that's all."

"I cain't argue that we got any further use for them," I agreed, seeing finally where my fool friend was headed with all this. "But we can always sell them. Do we get back into Kansas we can peddle them to some outfitter. There's probably buyers stopping every day at the posts, and any outfitter around would take them off our hands and be guaranteed a quick resale, the way hides are moving right now and not enough hunters out to meet the demand."

Chic looked sour. "Damned outfitters won't give us more'n fifty cents on the dollar," he grumped.

I shrugged and said, "Hell, there's no need to be greedy about it. We've already taken more out of them than they were worth to start with. Anything we get for them now would be found money, the way I see it." I couldn't help grinning. "Easy money, you might say."

Chic grinned back. "I guess you're right, Bert. Comes to that, why, we could practic'ly give 'em away an' not be losing anything."

"Right. So don't be worrying about it," I told him.

"You say the herd is just a couple days from here?" Harvey asked.

"Uh huh," Chic said. "South an' a little west." He gave the boys a warm smile. "If you boys've never seen buffs, it'd be worth ridin' down just for the experience of lookin' at them. Nothin' else like that on the face o' the globe. There couldn't be. An' Lord knows you couldn't miss findin' the herd. Not without you deliberately tried to avoid it by goin' another direction altogether."

Harvey looked kind of thoughtful. His pals looked kind of excited.

Chic stifled a yawn and stretched. He stood and said, "Time we was findin' our bedrolls. It's been a long day. Thanks for the chuck, boys. That was right nice of you."

I took my cue from him, and we both left the fire. We went straight for our blankets, but I could hear the low, murmuring buzz of the farm boys' voices until I went to sleep.

Come morning I was up early and got a small fire started. I was afraid I might actually have to start boiling some beans — which was all we had eatable in our packs — but the boys didn't let us down. No sooner was our fire well started than Julius Raskin came over hemming and hawing and toeing the ground near where Chic was still stretched out in his blankets.

"We'd be real proud if you fellas would join us for some breakfast," Julius said in an almost formal tone of voice.

I looked over to where the first flickers of growing flame were starting at their outfit. "Why sure, Julius. Damn nice of you boys. But I insist we should pay for the chuck we've been using out of your stuff." I reached deep into my pocket and pulled out the only coin we possessed, that double eagle that was the only thing standing between us and total poverty. I flipped the thing to Julius without looking at it.

He caught the coin and peered at it, and his eyes bugged just the least bit. "Twenty dollars?" he stammered.

I shrugged. "I don't think we got anything smaller," I told him just as offhand as I could. And, Lordy, but that was the natural truth.

Julius looked at the coin again as if he'd never seen one before. He stepped quickly forward and shoved it back into my hand. "Nossir. No *sir*. We couldn't take money for bein' neighborly. I, uh, gotta get back now. We, uh . . . you fellas come on over soon as you get washed up, you hear? You'll be sure and eat with us now?" He seemed right anxious about it.

" 'Course we will, Julius. We'll be there directly. An' thanks again."

Julius bobbed his head and bustled back toward their fire. He seemed in a bit of a hurry.

I kicked our fire apart before the illumination gave those boys too good a look at Chic's blankets. He wasn't making a sound, but it was a wonder. His blankets were just aquivering as he tried to hold back from laughing out loud.

"Nice touch, Bert," he whispered when he had control of himself. He threw his blankets aside, pulled his hat on, and then sat up and began groping for his boots. "I never would've thought of it myself."

"I was damn near too scared to do it," I

admitted. "What if he'd kept the thing?"

Chic stood and stamped his feet a few times to set his boots on comfortably. "Let's go splash some wet sand on our faces while those boys talk things over," he said. "No point t' rushin' them now."

We rolled and piled our gear and thrashed our way through the spotty undergrowth to the damp patch that was passing for a river at this time of year. Chic slicked down his shaggy bird's nest of yellow hair, and we took time to roll a couple cigarettes and burn up what was near about the last of our little hoard of tobacco. We'd been having to go awfully light on the stuff lately.

"Time enough, do you figure?" I asked when the last puffs had been pinched out of our smokes.

"I'd say so," Chic agreed.

There was light enough now that we could go back without worrying about losing an eyeball to a stray branch. The farm boys had bacon hot and ready and a pot of freshly boiled coffee and had dragged two cans of peaches out of hiding to have with breakfast. I guessed they wanted to put us in a really good mood. And I guess we were willing to allow that.

We fell to and chewed everything they put in reach, including the bulk of those peaches and all the sticky-sweet syrup that was left in the cans. The boys purely insisted that we have it, though we protested as politely as anyone ever could.

When everyone was tick-full and happily contented, Chic and I leaned back and waited. Sure enough, Harvey wasn't long in rising to the bait.

"Say now," he said, "you gentlemen were talking last night about selling your buffalo rifles and those Indian ponies, right?"

"Oh, I guess we were," Chic drawled. "Time enough t' think about that when we get back t' Kansas, though."

"Well lookahere," Harvey said, leaning forward. "We been talking about this. I mean . . . we don't have much money or anything . . . but Mr. Bert said your outfit was pretty well paid out anyhow, and. . . ." At the last minute the speech he'd had all thought out failed him.

"An' you boys thought you might try the business yourselves," Chic finished helpfully.

"Yessir," Harvey said lamely. The other boys ducked their heads. I imagine they were all feeling a little shamed about wanting to take advantage of a pair of wealthy strangers by getting such a bargain so cheap.

"Aw, hell, Bert, what d'you say?" Chic asked.

"I meant just what I said last night, Chic. And these boys have been mighty friendly. If we can give them a start in the right direction, why, I think it'd be a nice thing to do. You won't get any argument from me. Whatever you want to do will be just fine."

Chic nodded and turned back to Harvey. "That suits me too, boys," he said. "Now we know you ain't lookin' for charity from no man, an' we don't really need t' be getting the full value for our outfit. So you tell us what you think'd be fair."

Harvey shot a quick glance toward his buddies. Raskin gave him a nervous little grin, and Tommy Mabry was bobbing his head energetically. Harvey looked relieved and, when he turned back to us, a little apologetic. "Between us we've got fifty-seven dollars and sixty cents," he said. "Would that be enough?"

"Now that just wouldn't be right, boys," Chic said, and all three faces fell into embarrassed gloom.

"No indeed, boys," Chic went on. "Me 'n Bert ain't gonna strip you boys of your last cent. That wouldn't be at all right. We'll round that off at fifty dollars an' you boys keep the change for eatin' money till you start sellin' hides. If you got anything worth trading to bring the value up, that'd be fine. But no more'n fifty dollars' cash, you hear?"

Oh my, but that did light them up. They each one was on his feet and digging through his possibles sack as soon as the words were out of Chic's mouth. My gosh, those boys offered us damn near everything they owned in this world. Which damn sure wasn't very much.

Chic left them their knives — they'd need those for skinning buffalo, wouldn't they? — and extra clothes and food. He allowed them to press on us a nicely stitched set of leather hobbles, two steel picket pins, a pouch of cut tobacco, and a short-barreled Colt revolver, one of those that used metal cartridges, in a form-fitted, stiff-leather holster. That alone should've been worth twenty dollars, I would guess. And of course the fifty dollars in crumpled and greasy gold-back bills.

"Boys," Chic said when we were through with the haggling, "I surely do hope you younguns have every success in the buff'lo-killing business. I surely do."

We parted with handshakes and thanks and apologies and got ourselves the hell out of there. When we left they were wrapped up in admiring their fine Sharps buffalo guns and their swift, Indian-trained ponies. And, by golly, both Chic and me did wish those boys all the luck in the world. They were really sorta entitled to something nice for a change.

CHAPTER 8

We laughed our way clear into Kansas and by way of celebration had some beer and fried steak and freshly made apple pie from the new crop of fruit. Running into those youngsters had been purely good fortune, and I guess our spirits were pretty well up again. I know mine were, and from the way Chic threw himself — or maybe both of us, I don't remember all that clearly — into letting the ladies help us spend our money, he must've been feeling all right too.

A few days of that and we had a good start on being broke again. There wasn't riding work to be had this late in the year, but a blue-eyed and yellow-toothed bartender near the shipping pens suggested we head for Wyoming Territory if we had high, ear-warming collars and a sincere enough desire to make eating money.

According to this man, there'd been a power of stock cows driven up that way during the past year and a regular flood of drovers moving back south after the deliveries had been made. Talk of the high-country winters had apparently sent a bunch of those boys scooting for home, and there was a good chance that we could find a short-handed crew if we kept going north. So we thanked the man and headed that way while we still had money enough for train fare.

The good people of the Union Pacific were kind enough to notify us of our arrival at four o'clock one morning by giving me a sharp kick on the ankle bone, which brought me awake with an appreciation for Chic's intelligence in wanting that window seat.

I blinked and rubbed my eyes open in time to see the conductor jerk a thumb toward a dimly lighted platform on the far side of the window glass. "Cheyenne," he grunted.

I prodded Chic in the ribs and got a mumbled "mmpfhowzit" in return, so I poked him again a little harder.

He opened his eyes one at a time, cautiously, as if he was testing to see would they would or would they wouldn't work. From somewhere ahead of us the engine belched steam and you could hear the clang of the firebox door. "Huh?" Chic asked, almost alert enough to know he was doing it.

"Time to get off," I told him. "We done arrived." I got up and tucked my shirttail in and buttoned my coat and pulled my hat off the overhead rack.

Chic grumped and muttered some more but he got moving too. We grabbed our gear from the back of the car — bedrolls and assorted other truck bundled against the bellies of our saddles and tied snug with the stirrup leathers wrapped around to make it all one package — and stepped out into the night air.

We both stood shivering and blinking for a minute, hunched against the sudden chill. The stove in the railcoach hadn't been lit, and I wouldn't have thought that just being inside could have made such a difference, but I guess it had.

Chic grinned at me and asked, "What's the matter, Texas boy? Is that your teeth I hear or've you been hiding a musical instrument from me all this time?"

"Hush your mouth, damnyankee," I told him. "Your head's rattling every bit as much as mine."

This was the territorial capital and considerable of a town. Even at such an hour as this there was music to be heard floating in on the crisp, coal-smoke sharpened air, and lamps glowed warmly yellow in maybe a quarter of the business fronts along the main street. Chic nudged me and said, "A little warmer-upper would taste awful good, Bert."

"The hell you say. A couple more dances and a romp upstairs, and there won't be neither one of us able to afford a horse again. Then how'd we find work?"

We'd sold our horses back in Kansas. It was that or pay to freight them north, which we could not do. I had arranged the sale myself and pocketed the money from both animals. I knew good and well if Chic was carrying it, one or both of us would've been left afoot up here.

I took Chic by the elbow and steered him up the street. Not too far from the tracks we found a tidy, painted clapboard structure with the single word Eats painted on the glass-window front. There were lights and a few people inside. We went in.

The man tending to the stove was a little, city-looking gentleman with slicked-down hair and a neatly trimmed mustache and an almost fresh collar buttoned onto his shirt. Even his apron was clean, so I figured this should be an all-right place to eat.

The customers seemed to be railroaders on their way to or from a shift of work. They were wearing low-topped shoes and coveralls and some of those floppy little striped caps were on the floor beneath the occupied chairs. All of them were clustered around one long table at the back of the place, but there were other, smaller tables closer to the street end of the room. Anybody who wanted could have a table all to himself it looked like. I guess that struck Chic as something of a novelty too, and for a few seconds we just stood in the doorway and looked around.

Pretty soon Chic recovered. He led the way to a tiny, two-seater affair smack under the street window and helped himself to a chair. He tilted his hat back and propped a boot onto the saddle he'd dropped on the floor beside him. There wasn't much that seemed to bother that boy. I took the other chair.

The chief cook came over and made some friendly noises and asked, "What for you gentlemen this morning?"

"Whatever you got for breakfast," Chic said, "we'll take some of it."

"Oatmeal, eggs, and fried antelope steak would be usual," the man said.

"Did you hear the man, Bert? Did he say eggs, sure enuf?"

"You wouldn't be teasing us, would you, mister?"

"No indeed, boys. Real hen fruit, fresh from Nebraska."

"We'll take a double load of 'em, friend, an' that other truck too. We can gag down all you can carry," Chic told him. "I haven't seen an egg in six months or more, so don't be shy about breaking them."

He wasn't, either, and we each of us got away with an even dozen fried eggs along with the other stuff and a piping hot basket of baking-powder biscuits the like of which I hadn't had since I left home. By the time we leaned back for a smoke and a final cup of coffee, I was full up and warmed through.

The proprietor carried the coffee pot over for a last time and looked like he appreciated seeing people enjoy his food so much.

"I don't s'pose you'd know where a man could buy a horse around here?" Chic asked him.

The man eyed our saddles on the floor near his feet and said, "About all you'll find in town here is light-harness stock." He took on a thoughtful expression for a moment. "You might try C. M. Beasley. He's a lawyer and a good Republican. Runs some horses and cattle on a place about seven miles north of here, though he lives in town. He might have something to sell."

Now as far as I knew I'd never before had

business dealings with an admitted Republican — Texas boys are always taught you can recognize them anyhow by their horns and tails — but I decided it would be unfair to hold the man's horses responsible for their owner's judgment. And the comment didn't seem to have made much impression on Chic anyway. He was already asking directions to Beasley's home.

The eatery proprietor told us how to get there and said as it was just coming daylight we could probably still find the man at home. We thanked him and paid him and left.

The house wasn't but a five-minute walk away and not hard to find. It was built of sawed lumber and painted a gay and sparkling white. A matching white fence surrounded the narrow, city lot, which seemed the normal thing in the town. Although not so many were kept up as nice, nearly every place had a tight fence of some sort enclosing it, and after a while I began to see why this would be so. Those few that were not fenced had not the first bit of grass or greenery around them and on most even their porch steps had a well-chewed look about them. Pigs and assorted other scrubby animals wandered loose in the streets and the alleys, and you got the impression that at some times of the year, like in winter when forage would be in short supply, this could present a real problem. Anyone who hoped to plant a tree or a bush of any sort in his own yard had to fence the property or lose his investment. The few small trees to be found in the town were all behind fences.

The Beasley home, like I said, was neat and well scrubbed behind its fence. We let ourselves in through the gate and passed between twin rows of pruned and shaped rosebushes to reach the porch. A pair of wooden rockers were pushed back against the house front of the porch, and a chain-hung double swing creaked and swayed gently in the cold wind. You got the idea that the porch had been abandoned until the next spring.

We dropped our saddles on the edge of the porch and crossed the boards to the front door. There was window glass set into the door, screened by frilly, white curtains of some light, open-weave material. Chic raised the brass knocker below the glass and let it fall with a sharp clunk.

"Just a minute." It was a woman's voice, faintly heard from somewhere within the house.

A moment later the door was opened. And

I fell in love.

Lordy, but that was a pretty girl standing there. A little bit of a thing not more than five foot tall. Dark brown hair pinned up but not really dressed yet for the day's activities; curling tendrils of the fine-spun hair escaped from the pins to frame a delicate, sensitive, darling little face with high, rounded cheeks. She had bright, lively, sparkling green eyes under long, curling lashes. Her mouth was small and sweetly curved. Her frame was small — and sweetly curved. She wore a white shirtwaist and long, brown skirt. I guessed her age to be sixteen to maybe eighteen. And I would have to say that she was by far the freshest, brightest, loveliest thing I ever did see. Like I said, I purely and simply fell for her and before five seconds had passed.

I don't really know how Chic was affected right then. I wasn't paying any attention to him to notice such things as that. But I do know it is a damn good thing he is the one who'd rapped on the door. I don't believe I could've responded with word one when she raised her eyebrows into delicate, uptilted curves and asked what we wanted.

"We're lookin' for a Mr. Beasley, little lady," Chic said. He smiled his winningest, most easygoing, good-looking smile. "Is this

106

the place?"

"Just a minute, please." She returned a bright, sweet smile. She had dimples. She turned, still standing so as to block the partly open doorway but not shutting the door. "Daddy!" she called over her shoulder.

Entirely too soon she showed her dimples again and stepped aside. The man who took her place in the doorway was fiftyish but still in fit condition. He was nearly as tall as Chic and graying, a fine-looking gentleman. He was in shirtsleeves, but his vest was buttoned, his celluloid collar stiff and spotless, and his tie carefully knotted. He was carrying a large napkin in one hand.

"Yes?" Behind him I could see a flicker of motion as the girl retreated toward the back of the house.

Chic introduced us to the man, then explained what we'd come about.

Beasley took a half step backward and let the door swing open further. He looked us up and down from hats to boots and fingered his chin for a moment. A thin smile tickled the corners of his mouth. "Drovers, are you?" he asked.

"Top hands," Chic assured him. "Nothing short o' the best."

Beasley pursed his lips and asked, "Would you be looking for horses? Or for work?"

"It gener'ly takes one t' find the other," Chic said with one of those easy, catching smiles of his. "You could say we're after both."

The lawyer responded with a wide smile of his own, an engaging, politician's kind of smile that would insure some votes from people who hadn't been forewarned about the dangers of Yankee Republicanism. Come to think of it, I hadn't yet noticed how he might be hiding those horns. Anyway, he stepped the rest of the way aside from the doorway and motioned us in. "I just might be able to put you boys onto a good thing then," he said. "Have you had breakfast yet?"

"Just finished," Chic assured him.

"Coffee then?"

"Now that'd be right welcome." Chic stepped inside, and I followed.

I took my hat off, and when Beasley turned to lead the way back toward the kitchen I knocked Chic's off into his hands too.

The house wasn't too big, but it was surely nice inside. The furniture was heavy, deep-seated, comfortable-looking stuff with lace throws on backs and arms. Polished wood tables held lamps with painted balloon globes. The floors had been stoned and polished too and held a scattering of hooked, not rag, rugs. The windows were hung with curtains made of heavy blue velvet with gilt trim and tassels. The front room was really quite grand.

The kitchen was more comfortable. A round, massive oak table ringed with straight chairs. A copper sink and sideboards built onto the back wall with cabinet space underneath. Bare, stoned, but unpolished, wood flooring.

A nice-looking older woman got up from the table when we entered and fetched a coffee pot off the coal-fired stove. More interesting, the girl was there, seated at the table with a jam-smeared plate in front of her.

Beasley made the introductions. The girl's name was Elaine. A lovely name, that. It seemed to suit her just exactly. I hope it didn't seem that I was staring at her. Beasley took me by the arm and put me into a chair across the table from Elaine, nearer Mrs. Beasley. Chic he put to my right with a couple empty chairs separating him from Elaine. Beasley's place was between his womenfolk.

"Have some coffee, boys," the lawyer offered. "Some bread and serviceberry jam to go with it? I'll guarantee the quality. Helen put it up this summer." He inclined his head toward his wife. The girl's attention was on the table. She poured herself a cup of weak tea from a dainty pot before her, added sugar and a dollop of evaporated milk, and concentrated on stirring the mixture she'd created.

"Naw, the coffee'll be fine," Chic said with a breezy wave of his hand. There was a moment of silence. Chic nudged me, and I looked up. I'd been watching Elaine's slim-fingered, delicate hands churning with her spoon. Beasley and his wife and Chic — and now even Elaine — were peering at me.

I had to think back to remember what'd been going on. "Oh . . . just . . . the coffee will be fine. Thanks."

Beasley nodded as if nothing had happened, and Mrs. Beasley set a coffee cup in front of me and filled it from the big pot. That damn Chic was openly laughing at me. And Elaine, she had gone back to stirring her tea. I wasn't real sure, but I thought there was a wee hint of amusement rearranging the bowed contours of her lips.

I was proud of myself, though. I didn't blush, not even a little bit I don't believe.

CHAPTER 9

What Beasley had in mind was for him and two partners in a livestock venture to hire someone to keep water holes open through the winter.

"It's an idea I've been playing with lately, and with you two drovers showing up on my own doorstep, why, perhaps it is time to go ahead," he said.

The lawyer finished his coffee, cast an eye toward his wife, and pulled a cigar from the pocket of the coat draped over the back of his chair. He made a regular ritual of examining the thing, nipping the end off it with a vest-pocket-sized penknife, and puffing his stogie alight with a sulphur-tipped lucifer.

"We have open winters up here," he went on finally, "so cattle do fairly well when left to their own devices through the cold months. We have some loss, but nothing like the expense of keeping a crew the year around. Come February and March, though, those will be weak and gaunted. They come into town. Eat everything they can reach. But mostly I believe they lack water. I believe if we could maintain access to water for them, we could reduce our losses appreciably." He smiled. "Obviously, as an investor, I want to minimize loss."

Chic grunted once and I nodded to let the man know we were listening.

"We could not possibly justify the cost of a full crew," Beasley said, "even if we eliminated the winter kill entirely. Still, two men with axes — and a knowledge of cattle — might well repay their expense and something above that, you see." He leaned back, tucked his thumbs into the pockets of his vest, and smiled past the glowing coal of his cigar. It was easy to see how he would look in front of a jury.

Chic looked my way and gave me a quick wink with the eye that the Beasley family couldn't see. "We'd be willin' to listen," he drawled.

Beasley leaned forward. He spread his hands on the table and energetically said, "Good! Helen, pour us another round of your excellent coffee while these gentlemen and I get down to serious negotiation.

Elaine, you may be excused from the table, dear."

That did not exactly tickle me, but of course I had nothing to say about it. Mrs. Beasley refilled the cups while Elaine cleared their breakfast dishes from the table and stacked them by the sink. When both ladies were done, they withdrew from the kitchen with a rustle of skirts.

Beasley watched them through the door. When they were gone, he rose, crossed to one of the cupboards hung on an interior wall, and returned with a familiarly shaped brown bottle. He pulled the cork and sloshed a generous measure of the liquor into each of our coffee cups. "Now, boys, let's get down to business."

Well now, old Chic was not entirely stupid, and I hope I'm not either. Neither one of us was going to plunge into this so sudden. We rolled ourselves some smokes and munched on Beasley's fortified coffee — which I must say was awfully good — and waited for the Republican to open his bag of tricks.

"You fellows seem to believe you have a buyer's market going for you," Lawyer Beasley said when we were maybe halfway through the, uh, coffee.

"Just waitin' patient an' polite," Chic said easily.

"Why hell, Mr. Beasley, surely you don't expect a man to rush when the hospitality is so pleasant."

He chuckled and served refills. "I don't imagine you want to listen while I tell you how tight money is in the territory right now."

"Mr. Beasley, sir," Chic said slowly, "we will purely be happy to listen jus' as long as you keep pourin'."

The lawyer man held up his hands in surrender. "All right. No negotiations. Straight-from-the-shoulder talk. Okay?"

"Sure."

"Obviously I must clear any decision with my partners as they will be paying their share of the expense, but I would say that a figure of forty dollars per month should be reasonable. Done?"

I'd have jumped at it myself. After all, we'd been working down in the Strip for twenty-five. And forty a month was a damn sight better than nothing. Not Chic, though. He must have already had his mind made up to shake off the first offer, for he never hesitated, just shook his head.

"Nope," he said. "Fifty and keep."

"Forty-five," Beasley said without pause.

Chic examined his cup, found it empty, and allowed the lawyer man to pour again, without bothering with the coffee this time. I handed my cup across too.

"Forty-five and keep," Chic said, "an' you supply each of us with a personal mount. Bill o' sale up front."

"Done," Beasley said quickly. I wondered how high he would've gone if we'd pushed him on it. If there was a shortage of cash in the territory, this particular Republican did not seem greatly affected by it.

Chic grinned and shoved a hand forward to shake and seal it.

"I'll be glad to take your hand on it," Beasley said, "as soon as I have the approval from my partners."

"Fair enough," Chic said. "When will you know?"

Beasley shrugged. "A day or two, but I shouldn't be concerned if I were you. My partners are agreeable men. English, both of them, and very anxious to improve their investment opportunities in this country. Don't worry."

Chic nodded. He was prepared to spend more time talking about it over those tasty cups of coffee, but now that our business was concluded, Beasley was ready to get on with other things. He eased us out of there slick as a weasel stealing an egg and we were shortly back on the street.

"Now ain't that a spot o' luck," Chic said happily when we'd shouldered our saddles and let ourselves back out through the front gate.

"I would have to agree," I said.

"Yes, sir," Chic said. "Rich boss with a purty girlchild. Cain't hardly beat a combination like that. An' free horses to boot. Shee-oot, ol' Bert. Say, you still got that horse-buyin' money?" He knew good and well that I did. "Let's go spend some of it an' have us a little party, hey?"

"I don't know, Chic. If something happened to queer this deal — say if those Englishmen was to balk or something — we'd still need that to get new horses. Maybe we oughta wait a while."

"Hell, Bert, once we start workin' there won't be time for havin' fun. An' you don't have to worry about this. The lawyer man said so himself." He laughed. "This is gonna be easy money, old friend."

He took me by the arm and led me aside. Or maybe I should say he led me astray except in truth I could not claim to have done much objecting. And over the next couple days there, we discovered that while Cheyenne was no cow town and didn't seem to have much affection for cowhands, the railroaders and the merchants had come

116

up with some perfectly delightful facilities for the comfort and relaxation of a man who had a coin or two in his pocket and was willing to part with it. We got acquainted in a dance hall or three and saw a drama performed by a company passing through on their way to San Francisco and, in general, learned that there are certain advantages to being located along the road of a transcontinental railway, for whatever your taste you could have it supplied.

Our timing could not have been much better for just about the time we ran out of cash — and Chic got to talking about selling something to keep us going — up popped Lawyer Beasley.

"Good news, boys," he told us right away. "My wires were answered this morning. You are now on the payroll of the Second Son Land and Cattle Company, Limited."

Chic cocked one bloodshot eye in his direction and raised an eyebrow. "What kinda name'z that?"

Beasley chuckled and said, "It's in honor of my partners. Both second sons of families in the peerage. Remittance men, they are called. No hope to inherit, and no responsibilities, but their families send money. All that is required of my partners is that they do the honorable thing by remaining out of

England. So they live here — in 'the colonies' as they prefer to term it — and dabble."

Chic shrugged. I don't think he understood what the lawyer was saying, and I'm fairly sure he didn't care. Hell, I didn't understand what he'd said myself until some time afterward. Not that it made any difference anyhow. We didn't care who was paying so long as it came our way.

We got our saddles and other gear from the rat's nest where we'd been flopped — surrounded by grease- and soot-grimed railroaders — and tossed them into the wagon Beasley had hired to haul us and a hefty load of eatables out to his headquarters camp.

It wasn't all that much of a drive, and I began to have some doubts about what everyone kept telling us about the open winters in this north country. If that was so, why'd we bring all this food along? We had enough chow along to damn near make it through to the spring thaw without having to come back into town to resupply. All we would have to add would be fresh meat. And he'd thrown in a cheap, trade-type needle gun to take care of that. We were at the place by late morning and unloaded by noon.

Beasley's ranch headquarters was not what you would expect to find under the same name down home. There you would expect to find a house — maybe not a fancy place but some sort of house where folks lived the year round — and outbuildings and storage sheds and a scattering of pens for working and holding and breaking at least your horses.

What these Northerners had for their headquarters was a shack that was half dugout and half logs chinked with moss and mud. It held a sheet-iron stove and four bunks and a few dust-covered shelves and pegs pounded into the walls.

I'd heard stories about how the custom up here was to always leave a cabin stocked with food and wood for the salvation of stray passers-by. Someone seemed to've neglected to tell that to the last occupants of this place. There wasn't a scrap of anything burnable left in the shack, unless you count the bunks, and the only food was a jar half-full of wheat flour. The lid had been left off so that moisture could get in, and it was about as solid as well-mixed and cured plaster. I threw it onto the rubbish heap at the side of the place, and that completed our housecleaning.

Beasley stayed long enough to eat lunch

with us and then drove back toward town. He said there were fifteen head of saddle stock in a fenced trap further up the creek over which the dugout was built. We could pick out what we wanted to use and what we wanted to keep, and he would give us our bills of sale when we came in next. The rest we could turn loose to make out on their own until spring.

We looked around more when Beasley was gone. The outhouse was on the creek side of the shack, protected by the same cutbank that the shack was dug into and by a flimsy framework of warped lumber. Whee doggies, but I did know what a cold wind was going to do whistling through those cracks. That wouldn't be a place for sitting and contemplating come hard winter.

A more or less straight line of jumbled-together unpeeled poles seemed to be what was intended as a corral, but the only kind of horse I would trust in a rig like that and expect it to stay there would be either dying or already dead. Between that and the lack of piled wood for the stove, it looked like we had plenty of ax work to do even before the creek froze.

I shook my head and looked at Chic. "Maybe we should've held out for sixty a month."

"It ain't exactly my idea of a riding job either," he said with a grin.

Still, we were stuck with it. If we wanted those "free" horses, we were going to have to do something toward earning them. We sure couldn't change our minds now that we'd blown our horse-buying money in town.

"Let's take a look at those horses," I suggested. "And I sure hope there's something in the bunch decent enough to justify this mess."

"A dollar says I get a rope on mine afore you," Chic said.

"Payday?"

He grinned and held his hands palm up. "What else?"

We went back into the shack and got our ropes off our saddles. Beasley had said the horse trap was about a quarter mile upstream. If we were lucky, the horses would still be gentled enough from the fall work that we could lead or even bareback them down to the shack. I sure didn't want to lug fifty pounds of stock saddle that far unless I really had to.

Chic stripped the black-dirty rag off his left hand and threw the thing into the cold, ash-choked firebox of the stove. It had been a couple weeks since he'd been cut, and he sure couldn't handle a rope with a wad of cloth in his palm.

I turned toward the doorway, fiddling with the loop in my rope to limber it up some. It'd been quite a while since I'd used it. Besides, when you work with a catch rope, that is sort of a habit you get into. When you have one in your hand you just naturally mess with it, doing something with the thing if it's nothing more than re-laying the coils. I was expecting Chic to be on my heels, ready to go win that bet, but he wasn't. I turned back to see what was keeping him.

Chic was still standing beside the stove. His rope was in a tangled heap at his feet. His usually tanned and ruddy complexion was drained of color. He was staring down toward his left hand with a blank intensity.

"Chic?" If he heard me I couldn't tell it. "Chic?" I let my own rope fall and rushed across the room to him.

"Dammit, Chic, what's wrong?" I took him by the arm and shook him.

He looked up slowly. When his eyes came level with my face, it was as if he was seeing me from a far distance. A vague look of troubled curiosity touched his features. "I got no thumb," he said wonderingly, so low I could scarcely hear him.

I knew better than that. Hell, I was the

one who'd tied him up after he was cut. And I'd seen the end of his thumb sticking out of the wrap every day since. But I looked anyway. His hand looked just fine. There was a red and brown line of scab and new scar where he'd been cut, but everything looked fine.

"No, Chic," I said, shaking him again gently, "you've got —"

"*Damn* it!" he exploded, a surge of rage twisting his face and sending heat back into his cheeks. "I don't," he shouted in a rising wail. "My God, Bert! I can't move it. It don't *work*!" Maybe I shouldn't say it on him, but . . . quick tears of hurt and frustration had begun to well up in his eyes. "My God, Bert, what'll I do?" He was weeping openly now.

CHAPTER 10

It was true enough. Chic couldn't move his thumb, couldn't even feel it. It might as well have been a short length of stick tied onto the side of his hand for all the good it was doing there. I don't know what that single knife slash might have cut in there, but whatever it was had a terrible effect on Chic Robertson.

Now I suppose to a lot of people — say to a store clerk or a bank teller, even to a railroader or a hardrock miner — a thing like having a stiff and useless thumb would not have been a thing of great consequence. In truth, it would not have meant all that much if it had been my hand that was damaged. I would gladly have traded hands with him there and then if it had been in my power. And, Lord God, how I have since wished that that had been possible. I would've been glad to take an ax to my whole arm if I'd thought it would have done any good. Which of course it would not.

The thing is, though, that Chic was a dally-roping man and one who was more than ordinary vain about his abilities at playing a big beef on the end of a long, light rope. And to do that with the degree of artistry Chic demanded of himself, it takes a man with two very quick, very sure hands. You have to handle your reins and your coils, slip your dallies when the pull is too heavy, and lay them on again to tighten things up, all this while an unhappy bovine is going crazy at the other end of your rope. Do it right and you can play a beef like a fighting trout on thin silk line; do it wrong and you have a busted rope and a gone cow. Either way it is enough to keep a four-armed man busy as a mechanical churn.

With my downhome Texas style of tying fast with a short, heavy rope, it wouldn't have been such a big thing. If you couldn't grip with your coil hand, you could still drape your rope over it, and the horse work required is easier to get too since you can teach the animal what to do and then drop your reins once he's doing it right. I suppose you could learn to work tie-fast if you had no more than a stump to hang your coils on. But not that fancy dally stuff that Chic was so proud of.

This thing really got to him. More than I could possibly have imagined and more than was healthy. He never moved out of the shack the whole rest of that day. He didn't want to talk nor eat nor anything, just sat on the edge of one of the bunks using his right hand to bend and twist that useless left thumb. He never even picked up his rope from the floor, and eventually I coiled it and hung it on a peg with a spare shirt draped over it so it would be out of sight.

After a while, since he still didn't want to talk, I took one of the axes Beasley had brought out from town and went to begin laying in some wood. We needed a fire if we intended to have a hot supper that night. I had to be doing something anyhow.

The next day Chic still wasn't in a talkative mood, so I hauled my rope and saddle up the creek to the horse trap.

The stock was run-of-the-mill stuff. Ewe necked and scraggy but no worse than you would expect to find in the average remuda. I chose a decently made, light-bodied *grulla* for myself as it has been my experience that the smaller horses often have the most staying power. The grulla wasn't overhard to catch, and once the rope hit his neck he declared it no contest and showed himself willing to work. I saddled him and liked the way he rode out, with just enough buck to let each of us know where we stood with the other and then the ears perking forward with a show of interest and willingness.

For Chic I took a heavy-boned yellow horse. I knew he liked that kind anyway, and if he didn't like my choice he could damn well make his own. I let some poles down to take those two out of the trap, replaced them, and rode back leading the yellow horse behind my grulla. I turned them in to the excuse we had for a corral and spent the rest of the morning adding poles and rearranging the old ones so the thing could be expected to hold an animal.

I hadn't seen Chic come out of the shack even to go to the outhouse, and for a while I thought about working on through the dinner hour. But I had to go inside again sometime whether he wanted company or not. Besides which I was commencing to get awfully hungry.

The door was shut, of course, because it was staying chilly even during the daytime up here. Chic had a fire going when I went in, so he had been moving around at least a little while I was gone.

"Getting hungry?" he offered once I was in. It was an improvement.

"Sure." I hung my coat and tried to ignore the stifling heat of the place. It wasn't yet cold enough outside to want that much fire in the small shack. A dirt-and-log place holds its heat right well, and Chic had himself a pretty vigorous blaze going. "Lunch ready?" I asked, though I could see he hadn't started cooking anything.

"Just about." He shuffled over to the bit of shelf hung near the stove. He moved slowly, the way a man will when he's recovering from a really bad hurt. He hunted in a wooden box to find a butcher knife Beasley had packed for us and began slicing side-meat into a skillet.

It was then I noticed that Chic's knife was no longer at his belt. I never did find out for certain sure what he did with it except that he was quick to clean out the firebox the next time it was needed, and I never did see him wear a knife again.

I looked around some more then and noticed that his highly prized rope was gone from the peg where I'd hung it the day before. It seemed to have gone into the fire too as if Chic had declared himself permanently out of the roping business. I knew he could learn to rope tie-fast if he wanted, but I figured this would be no time to suggest it. Maybe I was wrong, but I decided at the time to let him ask if he wanted me to show him anything in that line.

The fire was overhot so the meat scorched, but I could not say that I really minded. I figured it was good that Chic was doing something again, so I kept my mouth shut and ate scorched meat and cold biscuits that he also found in Beasley's box — I kept wondering if Elaine had made them and they tasted better for that possibility — and drank coffee that he had boiled strong enough to make it good and then some. It was a silent meal but a definite improvement.

I figured if Chic was feeling up to cooking he was up to more vigorous things as well, so after dinner I got the needle gun and a pocketful of cartridges for myself and handed Chic an ax.

"I'm gonna take a look around, see what kind of territory we're responsible for here," I told him. "If I see anything worth shooting, I'll fetch us some fresh meat."

Chic took the ax and looked at it as if he'd never seen one before. I think maybe he was glad I wouldn't be out there working with the other one while he was trying to adjust to doing something without a normal grip in that left hand. That was the reason I was going for a scout, anyway.

"Firewood's the first thing on your list?" he asked.

"Uh huh. The corral is fixed enough for the moment anyhow. If it needs more, we can do it later."

"All right."

He started messing with our dirtied plates, so I went on rather than make it obvious that he was waiting for me to leave.

I saddled the grulla and rode up the creek to see would we have any trouble finding places where cattle could easily reach the water when we had to start chopping holes — it turned out there wouldn't be any real problems — and to see if the sheltering brush and creek-side trees ran far enough to give much winter protection for livestock. When I came back I had decided that Beasley and his partners had done all right in choosing their location, especially with so little wood elsewhere in the area. And I had the hindquarters from an antelope lashed behind my saddle. This really seemed to be pretty decent country.

Chic had cut a fair amount of wood while I was gone, but he sure was going about it the hard way — quite apart, that is, from any trouble he might've had with his hand. Since we only had the one rope between us now, and it tied to the pommel of my saddle, old Chic'd had no way to haul poles in close to the shack so he could cut and stack them there. So what he was doing was going to the standing wood, cutting it on the spot, and then toting the stove lengths back an armload at a time. I'll just bet he hadn't thought about that before he burned away a perfectly good rope.

"Evenin'," I said when he came staggering back with a final armful of cut lengths. I had already unsaddled and was giving the grulla a bit of a rubdown, which he seemed to like.

Chic dumped the wood onto our growing pile and said, "That yella horse looks decent though. I'll give 'im a try tomorra."

"All right." I turned toward the shack, thinking it was my turn to burn the food and I had best get at it or we might as well wait for breakfast. Chic stopped me with a hand on my elbow.

"Bert."

"Uh huh."

"Thanks."

"Por nada, compadre."

He smiled. Not his old grin but a smile nonetheless. "Damn Texican," he said. "You know I don't talk that stuff."

"Neither do I," I told him truthfully.

We ate and sacked out early, and if we

hadn't wanted to crawl in early from habit, we'd have done it anyway. There weren't any lamps in the place.

I woke up once in the middle of the night and thought we had a visitor in the shack with us, but it was only Chic. I saw it was him, down on his knees in a corner rummaging through his gear by the light of one of Beasley's matches, so I rolled over and went back to sleep.

CHAPTER 11

In the morning Chic slung a gunbelt around his hips when he got dressed. It was the outfit those Iowa farm boys had given us when they were trying to cheat us out of our valuable buffalo-hunting equipment. It was one of those handsome, late-model single-action Colts that fire a metallic cartridge and have about half the barrel length of the old-style cap-and-ball hoglegs.

There was certainly nothing unusual about a man keeping a belly gun handy. Nearly everyone did, although as for myself I'd never bothered to buy one if only because I usually didn't have that kind of money I wanted to spend on something I might never need. But having one tucked away in your gear was a whole nuther thing from strapping one on when you were off at work with your own saddle partner the only other human within some miles. Those that did choose to wear the things mostly only did so when they were in town. Or on the prod.

I looked at the gun and then up at Chic. I cocked an eyebrow at him.

"No one will ever again get the chance to maim me, Bert. Someone might could kill me, by God, but they'll do nothin' short o' that." His voice was hard and his eyes like glittering chunks of glass when he said it. There was no question that he meant exactly that, and I began hoping that Iver Cord never decided to travel this far north.

He crossed to the stove and poked some fresh wood into the coals of the overnight fire. He turned around and held himself sort of stiff. "You got objections to that?" he demanded.

I believe now that he was maybe feeling a bit embarrassed about himself, wanted to cover it with some bluster, but that never occurred to me at the time.

"Cross your legs if you got to, dammit, but hold your water just the same, Chic," I told him with impatience and maybe some quick irritation coloring my tone. "I hain't done anything dirty to you yet, so just wait until I do."

For just a lightning flash of time there he wanted to bristle but then he relaxed. His shoulders drooped out of the tight hold he'd had on them, and he exhaled loudly.

"Aw hell, Bert," he said, "I guess I'm just wound up like a two-bit watch, all set t' fly into pieces." He waved his hand aimlessly through the air and sat heavily onto the side of the nearest bunk. "Look, I'm sorry. Okay?"

"Of course it's okay," I told him. I grinned. "As long as you don't brood about it when you oughta be fixing breakfast."

He continued to sit on the edge of the bunk, though, rubbing the back of his neck with his right hand. "Yeah," he said. "That's the word, all right. Brood. I guess I done a lot o' that the past couple nights." He looked up. "I meant what I said though, Bert. Not to you, but . . . them others best leave me be. I mean that."

"Others . . . ?" I asked with a smile.

"Aw hell," he said. "You know what I mean. Don't you?"

"Sure, Chic. I know what you mean. Now quit worrying about it. It's just something that happened, that's all. You'll get used to it. Just give it time."

"Yeah," he said. But there was bitterness still fingering in his voice. I could say all the reassuring things I wanted, but for the moment there was no room in him for those reassurances to take root.

He pushed himself erect and said again, "Yeah." He began putting our breakfast together.

We went into town a couple of weeks later, Chic on the yellow horse and me riding the little grulla. And Chic wearing his revolver as usual now. He'd given me his old one, but I wasn't wearing it, preferring to keep it in my saddlebags where I figured such things properly belonged.

"Sure hope the lawyer pays us," Chic said hopefully as we breezed along at a brisk lope. It wasn't far enough to have to worry about being sparing with the animals and so we could enjoy ourselves on the trip in.

"Is it the end of the month yet?"

He gave me a queer look and said, "We've only been out here two weeks."

"I meant on the calendar, dummy."

"Oh. Damned if I know either. I've sorta lost track."

"Yeah, it's easy to do." Not that I really cared. It was enough to know the season. What month it was didn't much matter.

We were in town by midmorning. The first thing Chic wanted to do was go see Lawyer Beasley about the bills of sale on the horses and maybe half a month's pay. Funny thing, though. What with some window shopping and looking for a really clean watering trough and general rubber-necking, the poor fellow was delayed until almost lunchtime. What I had in mind was to catch the Republican at home for the noon hour. And maybe we'd be invited to eat with the family.

"Well hello, boys," Beasley said when we finally did rap on his door. He stepped aside and motioned us inside. "Did you come in for services?"

"Services?" Chic returned.

"Of course. It is . . . No, I guess you don't know at that," he said with a slight smile. "It's Sunday, boys."

"Oh. We didn't know, as a matter of fact," Chic said.

That explained why things were a little slower around town than usual. Not much slower, but some. Judging from what I'd noticed so far, Cheyenne was not what you would call a church-heavy town.

"My womenfolk are at services now," Beasley said, "and won't be home for a while." He pulled a hunt-cased watch from his vest pocket and consulted it for the time. "I, uh, have an appointment myself, but if you want to sit and wait a moment I can get your papers for the horses."

We sat at the kitchen table and waited while he brought paper and ink and pens.

He must've had a study somewhere in the house, but he didn't show us to it. It only took a minute for us to give him a description of the horses we'd chosen and for him to scratch out a pair of nicely worded bills of sale. He blotted them and handed each of us a paper and twenty dollars in hard money.

"That should make us current," he said briskly. "Just as agreed."

The lawyer didn't even ask for a report on the place nor what shape his cows were in to get through the winter. Of course it was up to him, but I think if I'd owned something I would want to keep track of it more than that. Another minute and we were back on the street.

"That sure didn't take long," Chic said.

"No free lunch and no beer either," I said.

"I'll bet we c'n fix that."

Chic was right, of course. That was one nice thing you could say about Cheyenne. There was no foolishness here about trying to close things down on Sundays the way you will find in some towns.

Chic was not his usual rambunctious self, though. He'd always been one to throw his liquor down quick and laughing and even quicker to throw his arm around the waist of a pretty girl — or as close to pretty as the

138

available selection would allow. Now, though, he stuck to the cheaper beer and was definitely impatient when I wanted to take my time about such things.

I didn't know why it should all of a sudden bother him to be in where all the fun was taking place, but raising some friendly hell is not the sort of thing a man wants to do alone, so before long we drifted back outside.

"I wanta stop at a store 'fore we head back," he said.

"It's all right with me," I told him.

He found a hardware store that was open, and for a moment I wondered if he was wanting to replace the rope he'd thrown into the fire. It turned out instead that Chic spent better than half his pay on pasteboard boxes of ammunition.

"We going to war?" I asked when we were on the street again.

"I don't know how this thing shoots," he said. He tapped the dark wood grip of the chunky revolver.

I eyed the heavy-loaded cloth sack he had tied onto his saddle and said, "You damn sure can find out now."

Chic had plenty of opportunity to practice with that Colt, and he didn't allow much of it to waste. Since we weren't supposed to be doing any herding, not even line riding, all we needed to do until the creek froze was to chop wood to keep ourselves warm over the coming winter. That we could do at our own pace. Or not at all if we'd rather spend a cold winter.

Neither of us was crazy about the thought of spending all day every day with an ax in our hands and a crick in our backs, so we gave ourselves plenty of breathing time between our daily workouts. I preferred to take that old needle gun and go looking for more meat to cut and dry whenever the ax got to feeling too heavy in my hands, but Chic stayed close to the shack and played with his toy.

He set some slabs of split wood against the cutbank below the outhouse and proceeded to whittle them into splinters one bullet at a time. When he got down to his last box of ammunition he set it aside and kept on with his practice: drawing and pointing and letting the hammer fall on the dead brass of already fired shells. Pretty soon he tired of just standing there facing his targets. He began facing away from them, to the side, any direction at all before he pulled, aimed, and snapped.

Chic had fast hands anyway, and all that

practice was like putting grease between two pieces of polished metal. He just got faster and faster. I wouldn't have rightly believed any human person could be as quick as Chic got at pulling that thing. It became a sort of game with him, and he talked me into helping. For a while there, he promised to carry the Colt unloaded if every once in a while I would snap my fingers as a signal for him to pull and snap the gun at me.

I quit that game after one day when I rode in carrying a pair of antelope hams while Chic was cutting more stove wood. Just as I reached the yard I remembered that I'd forgotten to bring the liver, which I'd been looking forward to having for supper.

I snapped my fingers in disgust with myself when I was still thirty yards or more behind him.

Chic hadn't seen me coming or known I was there, but before I had time to think about what I'd done he had whirled, drawn, and snapped at me. If he had loaded that thing while he thought I was gone, I'd have been a dead man then and there, and no amount of regretting it would've changed the facts.

But I think what scared me even more was this: I'd heard the clack of the hammer before Chic's dropped ax ever hit the ground.

Chapter 12

Elaine Beasley was never very far out of my mind that winter. Once the hard cold hit we were kept reasonably busy keeping water open for what must have been half the beeves in the territory, judging from the wild variety of brands that showed up along that creek, but whenever a chinook blew down or the cold seemed a little less intense we could chop extra-big holes, bury our ears in woolen mufflers, and run for town.

The lawyer man was pretty much pre-occupied with politics at that time of year, the territorial legislature meeting during the winter like they did and him wanting to keep the ice off the telegraph wires too by making sure the administration in Washington was fully advised on one thing and another, but I made it a point to keep the man informed about his livestock interests whether he wanted it or not.

It worked out just fine to my way of thinking because Beasley was forever flitting off to some caucus or council while Chic and I waited just as patient and dutiful as ever could be so we could give him his reports. And of course the ladies of the household were too polite to have us wait all that time without coffee or sometimes a meal to sustain us. It became the usual thing for us to have a bite with them and then help with the washing up while we waited for Beasley to come home.

After a few times, Elaine got over her nervousness at having cowhands visit in her home — I guess cowhands, especially Texans, were still unusual enough in the territory to be kind of nervous-making to the city dwellers along the railroad — and she started to talk to me. I say she talked to me because I was usually some quicker than Chic to grab a wiping towel when Elaine was washing dishes. Before long I was kept pretty current with the socials, the activities of the ladies' whist club and suchlike.

Early in February a group of the city's leading ladies began to organize a library, and Elaine's sink-side conversation became full of all manner of high-blown ideas and fancy language. I found that for a modest rental fee they let outsiders take out books too, which gave me something to do nights when we were at the shack.

But an awful lot of her conversation — when he was out of the room anyway — was about Chic.

"You mean you don't even *know* where he comes from?"

"No, I guess I don't, Miss Elaine. He hasn't ever mentioned it that I recall."

She gave me another in a series of questioning, half-amused looks. There was a playful, mock wickedness in her eyes. "You are just covering up for your friend, aren't you, Mr. Felloe? You don't really *want* to tell me, that's all. Why ah'll reckon," she said in a perfectly dreadful imitation of a drover's drawl, "ah'll just reckon it has something to do with why he always carries that big pistol."

She became more serious. "Why does he, anyway, Mr. Felloe? You don't carry one of those things all the time. Why does Mr. Robertson?"

I shrugged. "Most everyone keeps one handy, Miss Elaine. I have one in my gear too."

"That is not what I meant, and you know it," she accused. "Daddy keeps a gun too, of course. I imagine every legislator in town has one. Sometimes I think you men never do grow up, the way you have to have your toys and your bottles and . . . everything."

"Elaine!" Mrs. Beasley had come into the kitchen in time to hear that last part. Her voice was sharp enough to make her annoyance clear.

"Yes, Mother," the girl said quickly. But she gave me a conspiratorial wink that her mother couldn't see. "I *will* try to be good, Mother."

Other times Elaine wanted to know about Chic's folks. What kind of people his parents were, what his father did for a living, that sort of thing.

She seemed to have difficulty understanding — or maybe just didn't want to believe — that I wasn't trying to keep anything from her. I wouldn't have lied to her. I just didn't know.

I guess in her town-type world of polite society and businessmen and politicians and such, it was assumed that a person's background was a part of him and had to be known so you could decide where to place him in the scheme of who was better than whom. It sort of tickled me when I realized that she regarded that kind of snobbery and nosiness as being right and proper, yet at the same time she would be full of indignation and mental fire over the various philosophies of freedom. She was a regular bearcat on the subject of women's rights and independence and was especially proud that the territory had been the first to give women the vote. But she saw nothing wrong with picking a man's past apart so you could decide what to think of him in the future.

Me, I preferred the way it was down home. There no one would think of asking a man personal questions. We were interested in what he showed us instead of what he told us. His name was anything he wanted it to be, and if he didn't want to tell even that much, why, that was all right too. Someone could always make up something descriptive to tag him with, and at times a name like that would stick to a man the best part of a lifetime.

Elaine didn't see it quite that way, though, and she never tired of asking her questions whenever she had the chance.

I will be the first to admit, too, that while I would not have lied to Elaine Beasley for anything, it did not exactly disturb me that I could not tell her all she wanted to know. Except maybe that piqued her curiosity all the more. That I did not want.

The truth, I guess, is that I had begun to get jealous of my own friend. Yet so far as I could tell, Chic was not doing the first thing to try and promote the girl's interest in him.

It would be fair to say that at first he did not even seem aware of her. And I sure never relayed to him anything of her questioning. You could not say that this was deceitful or wrong of me, either. It would've been downright impolite of me to be getting into personal questions about him.

Later . . . well . . . no one could blame a man for taking an interest in a girl as pretty as her, and so I did not blame Chic. Later I became a sort of middleman, half brother to each of them, listening to what they had to say on the subject of the other one and answering what questions I could and trying to avoid having to give advice to either of them.

It was Elaine who told me most of what I came to know about Chic, for she liked to talk at some length about him and the tough times he'd had as a boy.

According to what he told her — though when he'd have had a chance to do that much talking in private I still don't know — he came from Independence, Missouri, where his father had quit after making a bold start for the Oregon country back before the war sometime. She wasn't quite clear on whether Chic was born in Independence or back in Virginia, the part that is now West Virginia, before that move west.

Anyway, Chic's father got as far as Missouri, heard about the dangers of the trip ahead, and decided he'd best take a nip to fortify himself for the ordeal. He was still building that nip to proper size when Chic left home, Elaine said.

In the meantime, Chic's mother had been trying to hold together a family that included Chic along with at least two sisters and three brothers. Apparently none of them'd had one thing worth owning in their lives and likely never would. Chic got fed up, left, and never went back.

From there, she said, he'd wandered up and down the big river from Fort Benton in the north to New Orleans in the south, left the river and got tied up somehow with a cattle outfit in western Arkansas, worked cattle in Oregon for a while, moved down into Kansas, and eventually wound up with the OX5 outfit in the Cherokee Strip where I'd met him. There seemed to be some gaps in what he'd told her and I believe some others in what she'd told me. I can't vouch for all or any of it, but it sounded reasonable enough.

Spring found our Republican boss with more time for listening to the reports that by now we were giving him at least once a week. It also found Chic with enough interest in Elaine that the few times he did visit one of the saloon chippies he did it on the sly to make sure no one saw what he was doing.

"Chic, if you feel that way about it, why don't you just give it up? I don't much care what a man does so long as he's straight about it, but this sneaking around ain't right," I told him finally. He'd just come out into the alley to where I was waiting with the horses.

"You don't know what it's *like,* Bert," he moaned, with more self-pity in his voice than I'd ever have expected to hear there. "What else can I do without it bein' a slap in Elaine's face? I swear, Bert, you jus' don't *know.*"

Didn't know? I could have told him everything he was feeling and a lot more. I didn't know, did I? Then who was it who had to run an errand out to the carriage shed for Mrs. Beasley and found the two of them cuddled red-faced and close on the buggy seat? They'd pulled apart quickly and laughed with relief when they'd seen it was only old Bert and not her father, and I'd had to put on a smile and pretend to share their relief, all the while knowing it was my own friend who'd put that color into Elaine's face and set her cheeks to blazing.

Oh, I knew well enough what frustration was.

"Face up to it then and talk to her father," was all I said though.

Chic snorted. We'd been through all this before of late. He took his reins from me and swung onto the yellow horse. "You really think a rich, important man like him is gonna give me the nod, huh?"

I didn't, but I said, "Why not? You're honest, aren't you? Young. You got as good a prospect as about anybody. This is still a wide-open territory with room for a man to grow in. Beasley doesn't care about cattle. You could handle his livestock interests for him and make yourself rich right along with him."

"You sound jus' like Elaine," he said as we loped north along the now familiar trail back to the cabin.

I could not argue with him there. It was her line I was parroting to him. I hadn't really any desire to give him any help on this point, not of my own, but she'd bent my ear a good bit lately on just that subject.

The yellow horse stumbled on the dark path. Chic snatched at its reins irritably and gave it a good cussing. He had a quick-burning fuse these days. "I wouldn't wanta suck off her daddy's money the rest o' my days even if he would say yes," Chic insisted. This too was old ground.

"You got any better ideas?" I asked sharply. I guess I was getting a little testy myself.

"Maybe I do," Chic said. He let it hang there.

"Fine," I told him. If he wanted me to fall all over myself asking about his idea he could just wait and be damned, I decided, for I was not going to do it.

We went a couple miles before he said, "Ever'body in town is talkin' about the gold mines over in Dakota." He hesitated and then swung in his saddle until he was nearly sideways, facing toward me. In a softer voice and one that sounded more like the old Chic he said, "They all say it's easy money, Bert."

Well, I wasn't going to laugh out loud at him. But I couldn't help but chuckle with him some. "Easy money, Chic? I never heard of such a thing."

"We could try it, Bert."

I could think of a hundred reasons against such a fool notion, and each one of those hundred would be another man who'd failed in such boom-and-bust rushes. A hundred men who failed for every one that made so much as a decent stake for himself.

Surely he knew that as well as I did.

"Please, Bert?"

I sighed. "Sure, Chic. Easy money."

He grinned. "We'll go back in an' tell Beasley tomorra," he said. All of a sudden he was full of plans and enthusiasm about it.

We'll tell Beasley, I thought to myself. And Elaine.

CHAPTER 13

If I'd had half a brain in my head I would've noticed first thing that there really *was* easy money to be made off the Black Hills rush, but at the time it did not occur to me, nor did it afterward until it was too late for such thinking.

This easy money did not come from what a few pan-and-rocker miners could pull out of the ground, of course. As always the big money in the mining would be made by the big mining money men, those already rich enough to spend a fortune for development and so make two or three more fortunes in return.

No, the easy money for the likes of little fellows like Chic and me was there for anyone bright enough to see it, but on top of the ground instead of burrowing into it. Transportation. That was the thing. With no railroads into that country yet, there were fortunes to be made by anyone with sense

154

enough to drive a team between Deadwood and the UP tracks.

Rumors about the Black Hills strikes were still flying as thick as fur at a dogfight, and thousands of men were streaming into those hills. Any sort of wagon or pack string could've been hired out at robbery prices to haul men and equipment up to the hills. The return trips could've been just as well booked with men who'd already wintered in the hills and were coming out broke and disgusted. The early arrivers seemed to be streaming out as quick as the Johnny-come-lately crowd was pouring in.

Chic and me had our own four-footed transportation, thank goodness, so at least we were able to avoid paying a forty-dollar fare — meals not included — from Cheyenne to Deadwood in an open-boxed farm wagon pressed into service by its owner.

Instead we were able to buy a few groceries and some tools and head out on our own. I say "we" bought this stuff, but in truth it was Chic who did our buying. For a change he was the one who had some money in his jeans, though always before he'd been quick to reach bottom while I fretted about carrying us through to the next pay. My money from Beasley had pretty much disappeared while Chic had been building himself a little hidey-hole reserve.

We crossed the rolling, empty, nearly dry country between Cheyenne and the Black Hills in the company of a regular stream of wagons and horsebackers so that never once did we have to feel lonesome. In fact it was too damn crowded. There was always a fire to stop at or, if we started one of our own, someone to stop at our fire willing to share coffee or beans or whatever they had in return for the company. Most of the men on that trail were Easterners, some of them so new in this country that they still smelled of salt air just about, and nearly to a man they'd heard enough tales of wild Indians that they wanted to bunch up in large numbers whenever the sun started to sink.

The talk was predictable each and every night. Not a one of them wanted to talk about the work of looking for their gold. They were all already spending it.

One little guy in particular I remember. He was scrawny and chicken-breasted, not more than five foot four and *might've* weighed as much as a sack of feed. Maybe not. He said his name was Theodore. If he gave his last name I don't remember it.

Theodore would've been in his late thirties or early forties, but his hair was already graying and thinned back on top until he hadn't more than a few dozen lank little comb-rutted strands draped over his scalp. He took quite a bit of ribbing about being safe from the Indians, but I don't think he took much heart from the possibilities in that idea. Every time Indians were mentioned he seemed to shrink and draw his shoulders closer into himself.

On another subject, though, old Theodore was bold and anxious.

"Now don't get me wrong, fellas," he said, "my Nelly is a good woman. Yessir, a *good* woman. No question about it. A Christian lady, she is. Temperance, too. Won't have the demon spirits in her home. No seegars, cut plug, leaf, or other form of the weed either." He took a swallow of coffee and rushed ahead before anyone else could break in.

"Not that I mind, you understand. I quit those things years ago, see, and I don't hardly miss them any more. But damned if that old woman didn't decide she'd had enough of my last remaining vice and pleasure, too, once she reached the change of life."

Theodore got a faraway look in his eyes and a tight little half-smile on his thin lips. "Boys," he said, "when I make my strike

I'm going right back to Utica. I'm gonna buy the house across the street from that damn woman. An' I'm gonna keep ten of the fanciest, flashiest, biggest-bustled hoors in York State there. Day and night, boys, and never a blind will be drawn on a window of mine." He went on in great detail describing just exactly the performances he expected to put on behind those open windows.

Others of the goldseekers were as elaborate in their dreams but none, I thought, quite so colorful as friend Theodore. Mostly the other gentlemen wanted money to buy farms or businesses. Some wanted to pay shipboard passage for their families from an older country to the new. One man told the evening's gathering that he wanted money to build a cathedral as a monument to the glory of the Lord. But he left during the night, taking with him a sack of tools and several dollars belonging to another man, so there were those of us who suspected his sincerity.

We never saw Theodore after that one night we spent in his company. He was riding in a slow-moving wagon that we left behind us early that next day. But I have thought about the little man from time to time and have hoped that he achieved his desire.

The hills were a joy after the nearly arid but heavily grassed country we'd been riding through. It was easy to see where they got their name, for they were darkened with stands of timber. A regular playground of forest and falling water and bare rock and fine, rich grasses.

There was more water here than reached the country south and west and you could see it in the quality of the new grass coming in thick and lush. Take hold of a tuft of those grass stems and crush them, and without even bending near, you could smell the sweet, heavy scents of it, and it was good. Hunt out a clump of brown stems left uneaten here from the last year's growth and you would find it still firm, cured on the ground and as rich as any hay a dairy farmer could make.

I'd never heard any man say that the Black Hills were worth a damn save for the taking of metals from the ground, but it was plain to see that this was a country made for the cowman as much as the miner, and someday I expect to be proven right. Whichever, though, this was a country to meet a man's dreams and maybe to expand them, and I was glad we had come to it.

159

I tried to talk to Chic about these things, but I do not believe he ever saw the hills in the same way I did. He was still likable. He was still my friend. But there was a reserve in him now that kept him wary and slightly apart from our evening gatherings with the others on the road. It was only during the day, when we kept the yellow horse and the grulla knee to knee in a roadwise jog, that he seemed to relax and let his good hand wander far from the butt of the Colt at his waist.

The winter of working with ax and saddle had not changed his crippled hand. He was used to it now. He handled his reins between his fingers with what had now become easy habit, and he could manage most camp tasks with a casual ease that would never be noticed by a stranger. But he still had no power to grip with his thumb and whenever there was close, two-handed work to be done such as the repair of leather lacings, the job was mine to do. It must still have bothered him, for he never would ask for help with anything unless we were alone, and he had long since given up his cigarettes in favor of a pipe that did not have to be shaped and rolled for every smoke.

"It's here, Bert," he said when we got into the hills. "Ever' damn thing a man could want, lyin' here waitin' to be taken."

"Yes," I agreed. But I do not think we were talking about the same things. He was looking at a clutch of tents and shacks bunched along one of the spring-running streams. I'd been looking at the grassy slopes beyond.

"C'mon, Bert. Let's go find a fortune." He gigged the yellow horse into a heavy-footed, rocking lope. My grulla followed with a less labored gait. The miles had been somewhat kinder on him.

Contrary to popular reports of the time, you do not find gold nuggets by searching the ground for yellow stuff the same way you would search out the mottled eggs in a lark's nest. Come to think of it, I really don't know how the hell you *do* find gold nuggets, for we never found enough to know what we were doing.

Others, men who at least had the appearance of knowing what they were doing, sloshed knee-deep up and down the graveled stream beds. They bent often to plunge their arms deep into the cold water, to scoop up pans of gravel and bedsoil and swirl the damp stuff with quick, practiced wrist motions. From time to time they would stop and concentrate their efforts in one place, storing the rocks and slushy muck separately to do something with it later.

On the more accessible and therefore the longest worked streams, there were elaborately constructed hollow dams to divert the running water away from pick- and shovel-dug holes in exposed parts of the stream bed.

Wherever you went in the hills, wherever the water ran, you found men. They waded every foot of the streams by day and at night withdrew into tents and pole lean-tos and — some of them — into hillside dugouts that resembled rabbit warrens more than human dwelling places.

Shotguns and long-barreled rifles were very much in evidence anywhere you cared to look. The miners tended to partner up once they reached the hills, one man idling near with a gun in his hands while one or more of his buddies did the actual seeking.

And they were unnatural jealous of their property rights. The least sign of color in a pan and one of them would jump to erect rock cairns or tin-can monuments, and thereafter they could claim a legal right of ownership to all the gold taken from their particular piece of stream bed. Already there were more markers in some parts of the hills than four times as many streams could've accommodated. No sooner was a claim abandoned by one group than another grabbed onto it. Markers were kicked apart, moved, and fought over with knives and guns and swinging shovels.

If I sound now like we were there as spectators in a gigantic tent show, well, we were not. Chic and I did our full share of toe-numbing wading and grass-root digging. In three weeks' time we found — by actual count — eleven recognizable nuggets. They were worth a total of eight dollars and thirty-five cents.

At the end of that time we were broke, our haul of free gold spent and our original stake from a full winter's work gone before it. The cost of buying food in those camps, or tobacco or liquor or anything else, was unbelievably high and the pickings awful low.

Still I do not believe we would've had any trouble beyond a few missed meals and a long ride south if that miner had not gone and riled Chic when he was in no mood to put up with such things. I don't know that, of course, but I really believe it to be so.

Chapter 14

We had left the run of one unproductive creek and were climbing the slope under a craggy, rock-faced hillside with the intention of pushing across eastward in search of something better. The ground was spongy underfoot with an accumulation of old needles from the limbs that scraped at our faces. If we'd passed any markers, I sure hadn't seen them. Of a sudden, though, there was a lean, dirt-crusted old man standing in front of us with a short-barreled scattergun in his hands.

"Hold it!" he barked, and the shotgun lifted menacingly.

The man wore baggy coveralls that flopped loosely around his thin frame. The clothes were as dusty as he was, and the knees had been rubbed and worn into tears so large the pantlegs were practically separated into short britches and denim leggin's. His knees, too, were rubbed until they looked sore beneath the gray dirt and ugly calluses that covered them. Most miners looked more wet than worn and were apt to be mud daubed. This man looked like he was coated with some kind of rock dust.

Naturally enough we stopped our horses.

"Fork over your guns," he demanded.

"Are you out of your mind, ol' man?" Chic wanted to know. He was stopped just ahead of me and slightly upslope.

The old boy grunted deep in his throat, a laugh that did not come out sounding too funny. "Not crazy enough to let a pair of claim jumpers into camp," he said.

"We don't know nothin' about your claim," Chic told him, "an' we care even less. We're just figurin' to go from here t' there acrost this hillside." He took a shorter hold on the yellow horse's reins. There'd been a time not so long back that Chic would've grinned and hung his head and tossed off some jokes and likely would've got us invited for dinner. Now, though, his voice got frosty and he said, "Move aside, old man, an' let us by. An' if you wave that shotgun my way again, I'll damn well kill you where you stand."

Hearing the way Chic said it, there was no doubt he meant every word. But the mining man wasn't one to back off either.

And a scattergun is generally regarded as being a most persuasive tool.

"Keep away, boy," the old man warned.

"We can go around," I suggested. "These people got nothing I want. Let them bother somebody else, Chic. We don't need the trouble."

It should have ended right there. I started to cramp the grulla around, which is something you want to do slow and careful on such a steep slope, and that fool with the shotgun had to speak up again. There's some men can't pick up a weapon of any sort without believing it gives them magical powers, and maybe he was one of them.

"I figured you'd turn tail an' run," the idiot said with a snort and a grin. He hefted the gun a little higher and sort of shook it under Chic's nose. It could, I suppose, have looked like he was fixing to use it, though in truth to me it looked more like a brag than a threat.

Whatever, the next thing I knew there was this thumping crash of an explosion — it sounded dull and almost muffled there among the trees and with that carpet of old needles on the ground — and the old man was running blood from a spot just below his throat.

The man's mouth worked, but no sound

166

came out. He had a puzzled look to him as if he was deeply curious about something and needed the answer right away. He went to lift the shotgun again, and again Chic shot into him.

There must have been moisture in the air, for the smoke from the two pistol shots hung in a limp, white wreath in front of Chic. The yellow horse buggered and almost lost his footing. He came slipping and lurching backward and shoved his rump into the off shoulder of my grulla, and for a moment both Chic and me were busy keeping our animals upright on the hillside.

From somewhere upslope we heard some commotion, and two more men burst into view out of the brush. Both of them carried rifles.

"Jumpers!" one of them hollered. "They've shot Morgan."

The other one didn't spend his time talking. He dropped to one knee and threw a shot at us. The slug sizzled past somewhere awful near, a sharp, solid-sounding THUP.

Chic's big revolver crashed a couple more times, and the second newcomer fired. By then, I had the grulla turned around and was skittering and sliding downhill like all billy hell. The horse should've needed eight legs to stay upright on that run, but somehow he did it. Chic's yellow was right behind.

I wanted to look back to see was Chic all right, but I hadn't time. Branches that had rubbed and pulled at us on the way up now were slashing and grabbing. I rode beside my saddle more than on top of it, ducking and dodging and throwing myself from side to side. I was trying to avoid the limbs and at the same time shift with the balance of the horse so as not to throw him down. A fall on that treacherous slope could've killed us both, and Chic and the yellow horse too if they piled into us.

Somehow we got to the bottom of that hill upright. I swung the grulla upstream and raked him with my spurs.

Now that I had a chance to look, I turned around. Chic was behind me, fanning his yellow with the barrel of the revolver he still had in his hand.

We were belly down and running hard alongside the creek, passing startled miners who heard the rush and clatter of the horses and stood to gape at us with their jaws dropped open and their pans forgotten in their hands.

Some silly son of a bitch behind us had heard the shots or maybe just jumped to a sudden conclusion. "Claim raiders!" he shouted. Although what danger there could be from two men who were fogging it away just as hard as their horses could go, I still do not understand.

Regardless, the damage was done. Just ahead, another man dropped his pan and hauled a pistol from his pocket. He had the thing up and pointed at my head before I knew what he was doing. I was smack beside him when he fired.

The explosion was close enough that I could feel the heat of it scorching the side of my face. For a part of a second, I wondered was I dead, but the grulla jumped a rock outcropping and I waved at the saddle-horn and knew I was not. The left side of my face was numb, though, and I soon realized there was an odd, empty buzzing in my left ear. I looked back in time to see Chic throw a shot into the man who'd tried to drop me. The fellow stumbled backward and sat down in the creek. I don't think he was hit bad.

Chic was shouting something at me, but I couldn't hear him. He waved his pistol, and I understood. We had to get off this crowded creek flow.

I swung the grulla left and plunged through the water. A spray of the icy stuff flew higher than my hat — which was not all that high, close as I was bent over that horse's withers — and came curling down over my shoulders. I pointed the grulla up the easier slope on that side of the creek and began dodging branches again. A few minutes more and we were over the top.

I pulled to a stop and sat upright for the first time in what seemed a long while. The grulla's sides were heaving and he was in a heavy sweat. There hadn't been time for him to lather, though. Chic drew up beside me. He was grinning.

"Hot damn *almighty,* Bert. We played hell, didn't we?" He sounded as happy as if he had good sense. He opened the loading gate of his pistol and shucked the empties out onto the ground. He dipped into a pocket and came up with fresh shells to reload with.

"I guess we did play hell, Chic. The worst of it is those people who saw us running. Now they'll think we really are claim raiders."

"Aw," Chic said with a wave of his hand, "we ain't done anything t' be shamed of, an' I'll say so to anybody that asks."

I couldn't help but grimace. "I didn't notice any of those boys back at the creek taking time to ask questions."

The breezy good humor faded from my friend's expression. "Anyone that throws down on us like that old man did is gonna get the same answer, Bert. They c'n kill us if they're man enough, but it don't come free."

"Dammit, Chic, I think you already did kill that old man."

"I sure-by-God tried," he said. "Hell, he shot first, didn't he? Tried his damnedest to shoot me an' did shoot you, didn't he?"

"He did?"

"I reckon he did. Look at your shirt."

Sure enough, there were a pair of small holes gouged into the side of my shirt and vest and a bit of blood spotting the ones furthest back.

"I never even knew he'd shot," I said, even if it did sound dumb.

"Don't just set there," Chic demanded. "Lemme see how bad it is."

So I unbuttoned and peeled the fabric back. It was nothing but a small scrape surrounded by a big and already darkening bruise. No worse than you might get from a broken stub of brush or tree limb when chasing cows, and I might have taken it for just that kind of nothing little scrape if it hadn't been for those holes where the buckshot had passed through.

"Kinda lucky," Chic observed.

"Uh huh." I worked my jaw a little. My

ears weren't ringing half so bad now. I'd been luckier than I had any right to be and hadn't even known it.

Chic started to say something but of a sudden he got the oddest look on him, as if he'd just curled up inside himself. His reins slipped out of his fingers, and it is a good thing he had taken to tying them together. They didn't drop all the way or he might've had a wreck. He was shaking like he had a sudden attack of the ague.

"Are you all right?"

He tried to grin but couldn't. He bit his lip and nodded his head to answer me. I guess it was the best he could manage.

The yellow horse pinned its ears and commenced a sideways shuffle that looked like it could be leading up to something. And I didn't think Chic's knees were up to riding out a storm. I moved the grulla a step closer and picked up Chic's reins from his horse's withers. He nodded again but didn't even try to speak.

"We'd better get along now," I told him. "Some yahoo might decide to break the boredom by chasing us over this hill. We'll be all right as soon as we get out of this area."

With that foolish thought in mind, I gave

the grulla a squeeze in the ribs and took us
both out of there.

CHAPTER 15

Since we had no money and no particular prospects — neither the regular kind nor the gold-seeking variety — and mostly wanted to get clear of that group of quick-to-jump miners, we turned and headed for Deadwood. We'd heard of the camp town, of course, but had not yet seen it, supplying ourselves sort of catch as catch can from pedlars and quitters and a little bit with Chic's gun. The idea of going there now was that where we could find the most people we might find a way to make a few dollars.

Chic was still intent on his search so he could find that easy money and set himself up with Elaine. Me, I was mostly going along for the lack of any better ideas. I was not exactly cheering for Chic's efforts to win that girl, but then he *had* saved my bacon twice now. Staying in these gold-hungry hills a while longer seemed a small enough price to pay for such favors, even if I would rather be getting back to the business I know, which is turning grass into beef and *not* grubbing in the ground for my spending money.

Anyway, we circled well around that particular hornet's nest we'd just finished kicking and headed east. We hit the stage road, by now thoroughly rutted and well established, that evening as it was coming dark.

"There could be a roadhouse close by," I suggested. "It'd be nice to sit in a chair again."

"We got no money if we did find one," Chic protested. "An' I'm kinda tired. If we got anything to eat, let's just lay up in the brush for the night."

I felt of the sack tied behind my saddle, but we both knew we still had a couple handsful of dried beans in there. "We'll lay over then," I said. There didn't seem to be any need to push, and Chic might still be feeling a bit shaky. He'd seemed all right during the afternoon, but he was the only one who could really judge that.

While I could not swear that this was the first time Chic had ever put lead into another man, I would believe it to be so. I knew I never had and never wanted to. It is one thing to hear or read about the taking of life, even to brag and bluster about what would happen if some so-and-so was to do this thing or that thing — but to actually pull a trigger and send hot metal into another man's living body . . . something like that would take a lot of thinking about. It is just too easy to see yourself in that other man's place and to think and wonder what he would be feeling when you did this to him. So I could understand how maybe Chic would not want to be among strangers this night.

Neither of us spoke of it, though, and if Chic was troubled by what he'd done this day, he kept it to himself and never turned to me with it.

We made a quick camp without bothering to look for water. The horses had drunk recently enough, and we had plenty with us for our own needs. We just pulled back off the road and flopped, doing our little bit of cooking over an Indian-sized fire. We'd eaten and scrubbed out our one pot and I was just fixing to lay out my bedroll.

"Don't move!" or some such stupid words as that. It came so unexpected that I didn't quite hear the words, just the meaning. A voice from nowhere floating out of the blackness that was gathering under the brush. I dropped my bedroll and straightened up.

"If you see the chance, jump behind them saddles," Chic whispered. It was low but calm and controlled, and it cut through my surprise. I remembered in time not to answer him or bob my head to show I'd heard. "We're standin'," Chic said aloud, "but we got no money. If it's robbery, boys, you've found poor pickin's here."

There was a grunt of sound from behind me and to the left, and the brush rattled. Another, similar noise came from off to the right.

Two men stepped out into what little light our fire threw. I'd never seen either of them before. Just a pair of mining men that could've been found on any creek in the neighborhood except that each of them had a revolver in his hand. The one to my right looked so nervous I hoped he wouldn't go and shoot somebody by accident. It would be bad enough to be killed a-purpose. To have it happen by mistake would damn well hurt my feelings. I turned so that I could see the both of them.

"That's them," the calmer of the two said. It was obvious he was speaking to his partner. He jerked the muzzle of his pistol in our general direction. "You're the two that killed Morgan Loomis this morning," he said. "Well, you didn't get away for long, did you?" He glanced at his partner and gave him a wink. "Two hundred dollars' reward, Benny. I told you this was them."

Benny looked more nervous than before, if that was possible.

Me, I didn't know what to do. They had us cold so far as I could see.

Chic seemed to loosen up. His shoulders relaxed and he laid on one of his sunshiny smiles. "Hell, boys, we thought you was robbers. Now what's this 'bout a killin' and a *re*ward?" He said it so easy I could almost believe it myself. Benny's gun barrel drooped and he let out a tight-held breath.

The other one was not so quick to be fooled. "Say anything you want," he said. "I seen your horses and checked those brands myself. They're just what everyone was told to watch for. You're the pair all right."

"Fine," Chic said. "But I'd still like t' know what you're talkin' about."

"I suppose those aren't your horses yonder?" the man with the gun demanded. He added sarcastically, "Or maybe you just traded for them this afternoon."

There was a flicker in Chic's eyes that told me this was exactly the story he'd hoped to palm off on the man. Without even a pause to think about it he said, "They're our'n all right unless somebody's clever enough to make a swap with us settin' right here at supper." He described both horses right down to their scars. "If those're the ones you mean, we not only claim 'em, we got bills o' sale to prove they're ours."

I think that kind of disconcerted the guy. Not for long, though. "Then that for damn sure proves you're the right boys, don't it? Well, the Merida has a reward posted on you all right, and we figure to collect on it."

Chic shrugged. "Suit yourself," he said, "but I never heard of this Merida. Who is it, anyhow?" Benny's gun, I noticed, was hanging almost straight down at his side now. He didn't seem so nervous any more either.

"The Merida's the mine Morgan Loomis and his partners run. Or did run till you killed old Morgan. Hardrock cutters they are and know what they're doing, too. They were just fixing to sell out shares to a syndicate and bring a stamp mill in here," the man said. "You boys could've messed up a good thing for all of us when you killed Morgan. If that deal falls through now, there's less chance for the rest of us to go over to ore mining. Have to keep looking for free gold."

Chic smiled again. "No wonder everybody's so anxious to find whoever shot this Loomis fellow. You say there's a bunch of money involved here?"

"Yeah, but I don't see what . . . Hell, you ain't going to tell me any stories, mister. You're just squirming like a worm on a hook, and it ain't going to work. You're just trying to feed us a line, is all." Which was the natural truth, of course, but a shame for the man to see it.

Whatever it was Chic was trying to do it didn't seem to be working, so I figured maybe it was time I dipped my oar into the water. Since he seemed to be trying to quieten their suspicions, maybe I could help.

"There's a simple way to straighten this out," I said. "We'll just go to this Merida place and see what *they* have to say about it." I turned and stooped toward my bedroll.

The man who'd been doing all the talking started to cry out. "Don't —" he said, but that was all he got out.

I don't know. I wasn't looking that way. But I'd guess his attention was on me just then. And Chic was awful fast with that gun of his.

There was the loud, echoing thud of a gun being fired behind me. I scooped up my bedroll and flung it backhanded at Benny before I took a rolling dive over my saddle toward the dark safety of the brush beyond. There was another shot, and I heard something fall.

While this was going on, I was rolling and scrambling along the ground trying to get deeper into the bushes and away from that firelight. I went like a damn black racer snake for about twenty feet and stopped so I wouldn't be making more noise going through all the dry and brittle junk on the hard ground. I was breathing heavy and had leaves and needles jammed into my hair and down the throat of my shirt by that time. For just a moment I lay there and listened to myself breathe.

"It's all right, Bert. C'mere."

I gave a long sigh of relief and noticed for the first time how heavy my heart was beating. Much more and it would've been popping buttons with each stroke. I stood and brushed myself off.

Chic was on the far side of the fire bent over the man who'd been holding the gun on us. Benny was on the ground right where he'd been standing, and it didn't look like he would be getting up again. "Gimme a hand here, will you?" Chic asked.

I went back — it was just a few steps — and piled more wood onto the fire so he could see better. I went on the extra couple steps to Chic and the man.

"Bad, huh?" the man asked hoarsely.

The fresh wood was catching now and it was easier to see. The wound was high in the man's belly, hardly a good place to be shot. Not that you could say there is any good place to be shot anyway, but this was among the worst. He wasn't bleeding much at all, but that was no kind of a sign. He wouldn't last the night, I'd have bet, and I don't know the first thing about gunshot wounds. It was just that obvious.

"It's bad, mister," Chic told him. "It don't look like you'll make it." It wouldn't have been fair to the man to be less than honest with him. He might need to do some preparing before he went for the Judgment.

"What's your name?" I asked him. "And his?" I nodded toward where Benny lay. "We can scratch out a marker maybe."

He turned to look my way for the first time — he'd seemed mostly to be doing his looking inside himself — and he sort of half smiled. "You'd do that?"

"If we got time," I said.

Chic gave me an uneasy look and then shifted his eyes away, but after a moment he nodded his agreement.

"Tom Henderson," the man said. "He's Ben Merle." He spelled both names, slowly and with great care. "I'd sure appreciate it," he said then.

Henderson did not seem to be in much pain. He was awful pale and seemed to be in shock, but he wasn't hurting. Not yet anyhow, and, if he was lucky, he'd slip over before the pain came in on him.

For a time, the dying man was silent but then, slowly and hesitantly at first, he began to whisper faintly into the cooling night air. I do not believe he was talking to us so much as to himself. Or perhaps to someone, something Chic and I could not see in that earthbound firelight.

Henderson was thirty-seven-years old. Somewhere behind him — he just called it the village, no more — were a wife named Ann and several children; he did not say how many. Budge liked rock-candy strings. The woman made cornhusk dolls for the girls one Christmas. Sister — one of his daughters perhaps? — was wearing a blue dress when he left. Loren was a good hand at milking cows.

He rambled about such as that for the best part of an hour until finally he could no longer be heard. His lips continued to move, but no more sounds came out, only sweetishly foul breath. Eventually that stopped, too, and he was still.

Chic's reaction throughout Henderson's dying was not what I had expected. Before he had been shaking and troubled and unnaturally silent. This time, though, he merely seemed impatient, as if he wished Henderson would die and be done with it and inconvenience us no further.

When we saw that Henderson had made his journey over, I leaned forward to draw his eyelids closed. Chic exhaled loudly and got to his feet with a weary groan.

"Are you sure you wanta bury these two?" he asked.

"I said I would."

"I was afraid you was gonna say that." He didn't protest, though. He found the horses Henderson and Ben Merle had left tied nearby. With them was a pack animal with a shovel strapped atop the cargo boxes. We took turnabout to dig two graves, and with my pocketknife I carved their names into green wood cross-pieces that we erected over them.

"Satisfied?" Chic asked when we were done.

"Yes."

"All right then."

He built the fire up anew and sat cross-legged beside their packs and the piles of stuff we had removed from the bodies before we buried them.

"My God, Chic, what're you doing?"

He gave me a quick glance of annoyance. "Seein' what we wanta keep, of course," he said. He was shoving their money and some other small items into his own saddlebags. I'd just assumed we would send it all to their kin somehow or otherwise dispose of it in a proper manner.

"Say, Bert, those boys had them a dust poke, too," he commented once when he was well into their packs. The poke went into his bags along with the other stuff.

I didn't really want to watch any more of this. I laid out my bedroll and went to sleep, but the last thing I heard was Chic rummaging in their duffel.

CHAPTER 16

I never did know just how much those boys'd had in their poke. I never asked. Whatever it came to, it seemed to make an impression on Chic, though I didn't see that at the time. The next morning we didn't speak of what all he might have found in their gear. We saddled our own horses and turned theirs loose, piling their stuff beside the new graves which I smoothed and flattened some in the better light of day.

From what Henderson had said, it might not be a good idea to be seen riding such damned distinctive horses as ours, especially that yellow of Chic's, but if anyone had questions to ask we figured it would be far better to stay with them and their bills of sale tucked away in our saddle wallets than with the less identifiable but still very much stolen horses Henderson and Merle had owned. Not that they'd stolen them, I don't mean. I surely do not believe that. But if we took them, it would be theft sure enough, and most folks tend to frown on people who can't prove ownership of their mounts when the need arises. And we still hadn't done anything that we figured was in the wrong.

"You don't still figure to go to Deadwood surely?" I asked when Chic pointed his yellow's nose in that direction the first thing.

He drew up without hardly moving anywhere, and the horse sidestepped and jiggered a little with an annoyed toss of its head. "Why hell, that's where we were headed, wasn't it?" he returned.

"Chic, there are times when I think you haven't got a brain in your head nor even a hint of one. If good sense was weighed out in gold coin, you couldn't afford to buy a cup of coffee. You heard as well as I did last night. Henderson and that Merle had us and our horses drawn out cold. And if they heard it, so have a hundred other men. Our best bet now is to slope on out of this mining country just as fast and as quiet as these horses can carry us."

"We hain't done anything wrong," Chic said stubbornly.

"I never claimed we did, now did I? I just said we oughta get the hell out of this country before we get messed up in more trouble. Lord knows we've had enough

187

already, and now Henderson and Merle are cold beef underground. They hadn't done anything wrong either. They just *thought* that we had."

"They brought it to us, Bert. An' I ain't running away from something we never done."

"I still think we oughta turn south and leave this country."

"By God, turn your horse south then," he said hotly. "Nobody's tied a lead rope from my horse to yours. You jus' do what you damn well please. I said I was goin' to Deadwood an' that's where I'm going. An' I'm not turning aside from anyone between there an' here."

He meant it too. He raked his yellow in the paunch — knowing better than to do such a thing but doing it anyway — and headed up the road at a brisk clip. There wasn't much I could do about it, short of cutting loose from him. And for a moment there I was tempted to do just that. Yet if you are going to partner with someone, you expect to take the thick along with the thin even when the thickness is in his own damn fool head, and so I followed along behind.

After a few miles Chic dropped back beside me where I'd been following without wanting to catch up to a talking distance.

"I s'pose you want an apology," he said, about half belligerent about it.

"Nope," I told him.

"All right then," he said. In another minute or so he added, "It wouldn't do any hurt for you to start wearin' that pistol I gave you. Everything considered."

I gave a bit of a sigh and decided against pointing out to him that if he thought I ought to be going around with a gun dragging down my belt, then we for damn sure ought to be going in the other direction. He had his back up on that subject enough already and there wasn't any point in bringing it up again.

And when you got right down to it, he was right. The right and the wrong of things be damned if it came down to that. If we had to fight our way out of something, I'd best be prepared to give my share of it. We pulled up and stopped long enough for me to haul the gun and holster and assorted pouches out of my bags and get them situated more or less comfortably around my middle. They felt kind of strange, and until I got used to having them there I was wondering if I was buying more trouble than I was avoiding by hanging iron on my hip. Still, I had a clear choice in the matter. If I turned out to be as much of a damn fool in this thing as Chic was being, well, I couldn't blame anyone but myself.

We reached the town of Deadwood that evening late, and Chic checked us into a two-bunk room in a crowded and sparsely furnished and none-too-clean little outfit that passed as a hotel. He gave the man at the desk a coin that must have been taken from either Henderson or Merle and used the change to set us up to some cooking done by someone who knew how. I will say that it was a welcome change from what we'd been putting together for ourselves.

Deadwood at night was a rousing, roistering, hell-raising kind of place, which meant that we could feel right at home even if it was gold and not cattle that had drawn all these people into this unlikely, lantern-lit spot away off in the nowhere.

You could wander around with your eyes open and see just about anything you had a yen to see when it came to the oddities of people. There were preachers and preachers' wives, whores and the gaiter-bedecked boys who touted for them, cowmen and businessmen, freighters and lawyers and engineers and flashily dressed speculators who were always interested in gambling someone else's money on someone else's mining claims. There were snake-oil salesmen who acted like snake charmers, and there were snakes who acted like charmers while they tried to pull a fleecing for the money in their victims' pockets. One thing you did not see a hell of a lot of was miners. They were out working. The town seemed to be ordered more for the would-bes and the ne'er-do-wells than the mining men.

If you had money in your pockets while you did your wandering, you could also buy just about anything you had a yen to own. The stories of all that free gold in the hills seemed to have provoked a host of merchants into stocking Deadwood with near as odd a variety of goods as could be found at Cheyenne, which had a railroad to do its fetching and carrying.

It was simply wonderful the ideas some people had come up with when they tried to anticipate the buying pleasures of a gang of newly rich mining men. There were fancy suits and pearl studs offered in abundance, silk cravats and fresh collars made of paper and linen and celluloid and some of enameled steel. You could get drinkables from trade whiskey to champagne and everything in between. One man with a suitcase stand was doing a brisk trade in Bibles and Testaments. Another nearby was getting good volume selling French postcards of a most imaginative nature. Another, more established merchant, with a real building erected around his wares, had an entire table filled with cast-iron toys and banks and doorstops. Who he expected to sell those to I cannot imagine, for come to think of it the people-watching department seemed to be considerably short on the subject of children. There may have been some of those around, but if there were they were being kept well hidden from the common run of folks on the streets.

The town itself was no great shakes, being raw and ramshackle and yet without civic improvements. What was lacking in beauty, though, was more than made up in vitality, so I suppose you could say that part balanced out.

Chic and I took it all in but were quiet about doing so, keeping our activities down to the drinking of a couple beers. Chic tried his hand at one or two of the gaming tables but only long enough to learn that this was not his night for getting rich the quick-and-easy way. We turned in early to make up for all the sleep we'd missed the night before. Come morning I stretched and snorted and took my time about getting ready for another day. It felt good to be so refreshed and relaxed again.

"And what would the plans for the day be, Mr. Robertson?" I asked as I wiped the last lather from our razor.

"Lookin' for a way to make a dollar," he said. From the tone of his voice he was not in half as good a mood as me.

"All right," I said, trying to be agreeable about it anyhow. "Ten to one there's some freight outfits needing muleskinners or some such help on the outhauls." I grinned at him. "I'll bet the biggest share of their help works one way only, from the rails north."

Chic didn't seem at all amused nor appreciative of my suggestion. In fact he looked kind of annoyed. "What the hell kind of job would that be?" he demanded. "Work your butt off in any kinda weather an' all of it goin' to make some rich man richer. Well we ain't going to do that, Bert. Never again, an' you can mark what I say there. I need that pile and fast, an' we're going to the top o' the heap or go bust all to hell an' gone in the trying."

Lordy, but he did sound serious about it too. He looked so grim and stony-faced that, for a moment there, he could've been a total stranger sharing bunk space in a crowded town and not the friend I'd ridden with and worked beside for all these months.

"Do you have any idea how we're going to go about this goal of yours?" I asked. I was trying to pretend I didn't notice the way Chic was acting this morning.

He shrugged briefly and said, "We'll come into somethin'. You can count on that, Bert. We'll come into something if we just keep our eyes open for it. You about ready now?"

I slung the towel over a convenient peg and tucked my shirttail into my britches. I already had my hat on. "All set," I told him.

Chic shook his head. "No, you ain't."

"The hell I'm not."

He pointed to the belt I'd loaded with his pistol and its gear — the bullet pouch and cap box and a nifty little holder for the powder flask. The belt and its weight of assorted accouterments were half under my bunk where I'd dropped them the night before. I had forgotten them completely.

"Yeah. I guess you'll have to keep reminding me, huh?" I bent to get the damn thing and strapped it on.

"You did remember to load it, didn't you?"

"I think so. Sure. Caps and everything."

"Jeez, Bert. You take that out like a farmer reaching for a hammer. You oughta work on that."

"That stuff I'll leave to you, Chic. I'll wear

the thing. If I have to, I'll use it. But, yeah, I guess I do look at a gun as a tool. You . . . seem to think of one as being a *part* of you, for cryin' out loud. For you that's fine, but it's not for me, okay?"

Chic clapped me on the shoulder and smiled. "Aw, hell, Bert. You're okay the way you are. Between us we can whup the whole world. C'mon now. We'll hunt out the biggest 'n best breakfast this town has to offer."

So we did, me feeling a little funny about wearing a gun in town like that but doing it anyway. Not that anyone else seemed to find it odd or even take notice of the fact. A fair number of men were wearing guns of one kind or another, and I supposed that more had hideout pistols tucked away somewhere. I would guess that maybe a quarter of the people you saw on the streets were carrying, which is about normal.

Breakfast was not quite the elaborate affair Chic'd had in mind. The only place we could find that gave its attention more to food than to liquor — which I don't mind at all, but not for breakfast — was a half-canvas and half-log affair with equal parts of dirt and grease and tobacco juice for a floor.

They served at a common table and didn't

give you much choice about what you had. You either ate what they put on the table or you didn't eat, but the choice wasn't all that bad. Fried sidemeat and boiled rice and some extra-light biscuits and plenty of thick gravy to pour over it all. So we didn't hardly have room for complaint. And if you could ignore the smells of all the people and the foods that had been there before, it wasn't too awful bad.

After we ate — it wasn't a place where you wanted to linger over coffee — we went out onto the rutted, dry-caked street. As far as I knew we were just ambling along without any particular direction, but pretty soon Chic's step quickened and he turned in through the door of a place identified by an old riffle box nailed over the entrance.

It was another of the town's saloons and was pretty much indistinguishable from the next except for that riffle box. I'd certainly never heard of this particular one, but from the certainty with which Chic headed inside I got a strong impression that he'd found time somehow to have heard about it and maybe to have been heading for it all along.

Inside it was your ordinary kind of low-type saloon, with tin cups and a very few cheap tin lamps and practically nothing in sight that could be considered breakable in an average brawl. It would take fire or a very determined man with an ax or sledgehammer to cause the proprietor of this one much worry.

In spite of the poor lighting, which the lack of windows did nothing to help, and the early hour, there was a good bit of activity around the makeshift card tables.

There were three tables in use and only one empty at an hour when I would've expected maybe some casual drinking and some verbal reconstruction of the night before. I couldn't decide at first if the games were run by the house or not. There weren't any wheels or other equipment around. Too breakable, maybe. Later Chic mentioned, though I don't know why he'd have cared enough to find out, that the house took a percentage from each pot.

The boys lined up at the bar for their eye-openers seemed a normal enough collection, but the ones bent over the spotted cards were a rough-looking crew even for Deadwood.

If I had to guess, I'd have said that *all* of these boys were carrying iron. Nearly half of them wore their hair long, which generally strikes me as pointing to a man who's a showoff or a braggart and sometimes to one who is downright mean in the bargain. I get along with most people and I'm damned if I'll back off from the rest, but if it'd been my decision to make, I would've sashayed right back out onto the street and found another place to amuse myself.

Chic, though, didn't seem to find a thing wrong with the place or with the people in it. He bought us a couple beers and headed straight for a table where three longhairs and a couple well-dressed loafers were seeing how fast they could make their money change hands. The stakes looked to be high enough that the trip around the table could be made in short order.

We stood and watched for a few minutes. They were playing poker, with which I am familiar even though monte is the popular game down home. Anyway, I had seen the game before but never the way these boys were playing it. Cold-eyed and tight-lipped and high stakes. They hadn't come here for any pleasant relaxation.

I was some kind of surprised, then, when Chic bought into the game not fifteen minutes after we walked in the door. He pulled Henderson's dust poke out of a pocket and flopped it onto the table. I mumbled something — I don't remember what — and went out to see if I could find all the sights Deadwood had to offer.

CHAPTER 17

It is kind of odd that I liked Deadwood as much as I did. Odd because for one thing it was a mud-colored gulch filled with miners and their destruction. Odder still because it was so enclosed by the steep hills and rock faces that hung about it. As a rule I prefer a bigger, flatter, more open country with more in the way of grass on it. In spite of that, though, there was something about the place that made me disregard those bad features more than normal. Maybe it was that I was starting to relax again after the troubles we'd just come through.

I spent a little time idling in a dry-goods store that the owner had taken the bother to build solidly of squared logs. He either had to've been among the first into the gulch or had hauled his timbers from elsewhere, for there sure was nothing left in the way of standing wood and did not look like there had been any lately. Miners seem to have a peculiar ability to turn forest into mud practically overnight.

Later on I stopped outside a much-smeared, long-ago-white tent to listen to a preacher man expound on the evils of strong drink and strong tobacco. From what I'd seen so far, he had plenty of room to work his way upward from there on the scale of Deadwood's vices, but maybe he had just begun his battle plan here. Whatever, he had a good voice and was interesting to listen to.

When he paused for breath and it wouldn't seem too impolite, I left and nosed into a few of the smaller saloons and into one downright grandiose one with a pair of glass chandeliers hung above the bar and globe lamps around the walls. I must not have looked very presentable by their standards, though, for I quickly got a cold-eyed stare that let me know I should go elsewhere.

I had twelve cents left in my pockets and a dime would buy you a beer — it's true, they charged that much for a single beer there — and I decided I might as well spend my money and be done with it. I stepped around to the nearest other place after leaving the fancy bar and walked inside.

It seemed a nice enough saloon, the floors

cleanly raked and empty tin cans spotted around in convenient locations for those who chewed. There wasn't much in the way of sit-down facilities, the few tables and stools being occupied by card players. Most of the boys in the room, which was wood walled but canvas roofed, stood along the bar in scattered clumps where they could keep an eye on the progress of the games.

The bartender took my dime and exchanged it for a tin mug of beer with just enough head on it to show it was good. In spite of the price he charged, he wasn't trying to gouge anyone with a short measure. I leaned against the rough wood bar and sipped at my beer and was satisfied with the drink and the day and the prospects for the future. Before long, Chic should get tired of Deadwood and we could drift back to the short-grass country, maybe back over to Wyoming where the grass just has to be seen to be believed, and we could go back to work.

I was standing there like that, sipping my beer and thinking pleasant thoughts, when someone stumbled and smashed into my side. It jostled my arm and sent a neatly curling arc of golden beer into the air to splash wetly against my chest. It was reason enough for a surge of anger I suppose, but I was in a good humor and didn't even mind that the man who'd had the accident stood looking at me without apology. It would dry and no harm done.

But then the silly sonuvabitch reached out and shoved my arm again. He got a smaller splash of beer down my shirt front. I would have to say that I was not so willing to discount that as an accident.

"Mister, this here beer was bought with my last dime. I'll thank you to wait while I finish it, and then maybe we can discuss your manners."

He gave me a slow, twisty grin and bobbed his head. He stepped back a pace and stood eying me.

I took another swallow of the beer and eyeballed him right back over the rim of the mug. I was half expecting him to lunge when I had the cup tilted and was ready for it if he did, but he stood still.

Who he was or what he wanted I could not imagine. I'm sure I had never seen him before. He was a middling-tall man, maybe a couple inches taller than me, and very dark. Straight black hair that needed cutting, heavy mustache, dark beard stubble, deep-set dark brown eyes under thick brows, and a well-weathered complexion. He was wearing jeans and jackboots and a nearly new red shirt and had a knife at his belt. If he was wearing a gun, it didn't show. There was something in his expression that said this was a man who thought himself meaner and leaner and tougher than he really was.

Now I've never made claims to being much of a rough-and-tumble heller, but you just can't hardly wrestle steers without learning how to move and you can't hardly handle them either without building a little muscle. And I learned early that one of the best ways to live peaceably among rough men is to never back off from one of them. When they know you're willing and able, they tend to leave you alone as being the more comfortable course of action. So I was not going to tremble and whimper just because this character wanted himself some exercise.

I gave the man a little salute with my mug and drained off the last of the beer he'd left me. "What now, mister?"

Again he grinned. He took his knife from its sheath and laid it carefully onto the bar. He was establishing the rules, and that was all right with me. I fished my pistol out of the holster and laid it beside the knife. The bartender was thoughtful enough to take both of them and move them to a shelf well out of reach behind the bar. One got the idea this was not a highly unusual happening.

The man apparently wanted to crow and brag and thump on his chest a while before he stomped on me. Still grinning, he stepped forward and began to tell me just how very bad he was. I don't know what all he was saying, for I wasn't hardly listening. In the middle of whatever it was he was saying, I up and smashed him a good one with my right.

The quickness of it must have surprised him, for he never even tried to jerk his head away. The flat of my knuckles landed with a most gratifying whap and my chum had himself a nicely split lip that began running blood right smartly.

Too late, he decided to duck and throw a hand up to protect his face. Well, since he'd made me a present of it, I accepted. I shuffled forward, feinted high again with my right and slipped a low, hard left in under his arms to that wind pocket that lies between belly and chest. You could hear the breath whoosh out of him, and he began to look a bit pale. And a hell of a lot less cocky. He was discovering that I wasn't going to roll over and play dead just on his say-so. Whatever he got here he'd have to pay for.

Seeing as he'd laid down civilized rules

about this and we seemed to be in it for the fun of it, I stepped back and let him get his breath.

The color came back to his face and the heaving he was doing trying to catch his breath seemed to lessen a little. He shook his head and stepped toward me again but more warily now. He wasn't grinning this time.

Whatever else I might want to say about the man, he did move pretty well, and he was sure enough on his guard now. He did a fast shuffle with his feet and launched a hard, looping right. I had no trouble plucking his right out of the air and sending it harmlessly off to the side, but along about then a short, straight left thudded solidly into my right cheek. Where it came from I never did see.

His punch stung sure enough, but there is something about me that doesn't really get into the proper feel of a fight until I've taken that first one. Until then I'm a little reluctant to really get in and mix it up. Once I get rocked, though, I can remember that it only hurts so much and can get on with the business at hand.

Anyway, we were both ready now and for a little while moused around in front of each other, jabbing and blocking by turns but neither doing much in the way of damage. It had been a long time since I'd done anything like this, and I was commencing to really enjoy it.

The spectators in the place had left off watching the card games and were ringed close around us now. I was dimly aware of them and could sort of half hear several people shouting encouragement to their favorite, mostly under the name of Roy. That was all right until one son of a bitch decided to give his support in a more positive way and jabbed me a solid shot over the kidney. I stepped back into him with an elbow in the gut, which solved that problem but left me open to a heel-jarring smash from Roy's left again.

I began to get a bit mad after that — he could see perfectly well what I was doing and could've held off a moment — so I stepped up the pace. Roy was pretty good at blocking one at a time, but I found that I could confuse him considerable by raining them on him hard and often. Within another minute his face was cut up and bloody.

He must have been feeling a little desperate before his hometown audience, for of a sudden he brought a knee flashing up toward my groin. I just barely had time to twist away and catch it on the thigh and at that it hurt like hell. That put a mad on me for fair.

I quit fighting for the fun of it then and moved in closer. I gave up a couple glancing blows to the head, one of them solid enough to send a warm flow of blood down onto my collar, but in return I buried four solid ones low in Roy's belly. That was enough to finish the job I'd started on his wind and to put some lead weights into his arms. I backed off again and began sailing rights in over his guard to land high on the jaw.

I doubt he was seeing any more out of that left eye, and my right hand was starting to puff. It was time to end it. Again I stepped close and ripped a couple combinations into his gut. As soon as his hands came down I moved back, took half a moment to pick my spot, and laid all I had onto the left shelf of his jaw. It was enough. His eyes went out of focus and his knees sagged. When he didn't go down right away, I gave him a second helping from the same dish. This time he hit the floor.

I stepped back. I was tireder, sweatier, and bloodier than I'd realized. Some fool kept slapping me on the back, which hurt damn near as much as anything Roy'd been able to do. Someone else — I liked him better, whoever he was — shoved a mug of beer into my hands. I was shaking so much I like to spilled it, but I got it where it needed to be and it tasted just fine.

Everyone seemed to think I'd just done something real strange. They pretty well ignored Roy as he crawled back onto his feet, shaking his head and mopping blood from the cuts on his face.

Now the normal way to do things, or at least what I would've done had it been me down there chewing sawdust, would've been for the loser to force a phony smile and shake hands and offer to buy the next beer — try to salvage something out of it anyhow. Not Roy. He stood with his chin lowered, staring real venom past those dark and bushy and now blood-matted eyebrows. He never said a word to me and after an awkward moment he turned and walked away. I would have to admit to being pleased then to see that he was none too steady on his feet even yet.

CHAPTER 18

Chic joined me at our room at suppertime, which was a damn good thing. I hadn't money to buy a meal myself and in this place you paid for your room and your eating separate. And I was some kind of ready to eat, too, after the morning's exercise and having lunched off no more than a couple deep-drawn breaths of the high, clean air.

At least the air here was still untainted by the miners and their mud. It was clean, with just a pleasantly biting tinge of wood smoke from the dozens and maybe hundreds of cooking fires up and down the maze of gulches at and near the camp.

Chic was in a good humor and just a wee bit drunk. He never said but, from the mood he was in, I figured he must have done some winning at his cards. Which was fine by me. I wanted myself a helluva big supper this night and he was the lad who'd have to be paying for it.

It strikes me odd to think of it now, but at the time I never gave a worry any longer to where that money had come from. I guess I just plain had put that out of my mind, which is a thing I'm afraid I sometimes do with unpleasant subjects.

Anyhow, we found ourselves a real uptown eatery, a place built all of sawn lumber that had to have been hauled in piecemeal from some other place, for so far I had seen no indications of there being a sawmill any-where in these hills.

The place was clean and, wonder of wonders, it also was serving fresh beef. Most beaneries in the country at the time had nothing but dried or salted beef and little enough of that. For the most part these mining men ate pork, smoked and heavy salted, not really the thing for a man who knows the taste of good, sturdy, grass-fed beef.

Chic was as delighted as me to see what was available. He ordered us a pair of thick, tallow-fried steaks, and the man in the apron did such a good job of cooking them that I wondered if he might've been a Texas man gone near to rack and ruin in this cow-less country. When I asked, though, he said he was from Illinois. Which makes one wonder. Whatever, it was one hell of a fine meal.

Afterward we went back to Chic's favorite saloon, and he jumped right back into the play. This time when he rapped his poke onto the table, though, it sounded considerable lighter than it had earlier in the day. That surprised me, considering the fine mood he'd been in all through dinner. Since I hadn't anything better to do, I idled nearby and watched.

"Jacks or better to open, gentlemen, and the game is draw."

"Draw two."

"Hit me for one here, fella."

"Dealer stands pat."

The words were a low, droning murmur that rolled together in an emotionless flow of sounds. Chic won a small pot, lost another, and lost more heavily on a third. If he had anything at all in his hand, he seemed to want to stay in as deep as it took to buy a look at the other players' cards. It seemed foolish to my way of thinking, but then I am not much of a gambling man. And the next hand was one that Chic raked in. He must have made more than twenty dollars beyond what he'd put in himself to build it that far. He was fairly beaming after that and switched off of beer to begin drinking a rum concoction of some sort. I had a couple more beers myself and went on to bed, leaving Chic to his own pursuits.

I woke up in a fine frame of mind, having slept so sound I never heard Chic come in during the night. When I shook him out of his blankets, he was bleary-eyed and had a stale smell about him.

"What the hell time 'zit?" he wanted to know.

"It's breaking day, you lazy bastard. Time to be up and busy again."

He sat up and knuckled his eyes and ran a hand over his beard stubble. He cussed to himself a little and went to lie back down, so I took my pillow and flailed him over the head a few times. He grinned and sat back up and shook his head. "All right, dammit. I'm awake."

I hit him one more time to make sure and got our shaving gear off the shelf. I lathered up and let it work while I sat to strop the razor against the side of my boot.

"I found us a job t' do," Chic said just as I was ready to make my first cut.

I dropped my hand and spun around. "Jeez, that's great." I couldn't help asking, "Easy money?"

Chic laughed. "What else?" He began getting dressed. "Actually it should be real easy. Easy enough for a dumb ol' boy like you, Bert. Jus' make a delivery of some horses gentle enough for a military lead."

"Sounds good to me," I told him. I went back to my shaving feeling downright good about our prospects and managed to get through the entire procedure without once cutting a pocket into my cheek, which I sometimes do. I swear if I could stand the itching long enough I'd grow myself a beard and give up shaving altogether.

"We'll leave in a couple days," he said. "Pick up the horses south o' here, carry 'em down into the grass hills for delivery. Shouldn't be hardly anything to it."

"I'm ready whenever you say," I told him. I wiped off the last of the lather and handed him our soap and brush and razor. "How's about a celebration breakfast whenever you fin'ly get presentable enough to appear in public?"

Chic fingered his chin in a way that had nothing to do with shaving and gave me a rueful little half-smile. "Yeah, if you don't spend too heavy. We . . . uh . . . got a twenty-buck advance in pay t' last us 'til this job is done."

I just had to laugh at him. "Lost pretty heavy, did you?"

"Wiped out jus' prettier'n hell, Bert. You

213

ain't mad?"

"Mad? What for? Of course I'm not mad. That sort of thing happens to everybody now and then. No, I ain't mad at you."

The simple truth was that I was pleased. Considering where that money had come from, I figured we were better off not being burdened by it. And I suspected that that sort of thinking hidden away down inside might've been why Chic had played such really awful poker the night before. For it is a fact that bad money will not do you the least bit of good. Throw it away on cards or whatever and you haven't lost a thing of any value. Whatever, I was glad that what Chic had now was money we'd be earning fair and square and could consider to be ours.

That being the case I did not at all mind going light on the spending again. Hell, that was what I'd been used to for as long as I could remember anyhow. I wasn't going to get excited about having to do it now.

So we went and found ourselves a cheap and easy greasy-spoon kind of place where for fifty cents a head — the least you could find in the gulch it was, too — a body could tuck into all he wanted of such go-far items as oatmeal, cornbread, and beans plus get a four-chunk serving of bacon at breakfast time or a two-slice plate of ham the rest of the day. Other than that, these people never changed their menu, as we were to discover over the next couple days. And let me tell you, by then I was pretty tired of eating dried-out cornbread and slimy, slick oatmeal and overcooked beans that they never put enough onion into.

Chic stayed away from the gambling houses after that, though, and we amused ourselves by doing some wall picking in search of a good vein that everyone else might've overlooked when they were claiming the whole area the first time through. The odds on us finding anything — and the outcome — were about what you might expect. Still, it gave us something to do since we couldn't afford any of Deadwood's more costly pastimes. Unfortunately.

After three days of that, Chic disappeared during the afternoon and came back in a rush to gather some supplies and get to moving. Which we did.

The horses were on their toes and feeling feisty after being so little used, and it felt good to be having it out with a cold-backed animal again.

That grulla let me know what was up as soon as I stepped into the pen with the rope in my hand. He pretended to be paying me no attention, but his ears pinned back immediately I let myself through the gate, and he brought his weight down square onto all four legs from the rump-twisted way he'd been standing until then.

I foxed him, though. I took my time building a loop, laid it out, and flipped it not at him but onto the yellow standing nearby. The grulla flinched anyway when he saw the loop flying, and I'd swear that it made him mad when he saw the mistake he'd made. I sat back hard on the yella, which was as startled as my grulla'd been prepared to be, and handed him over to Chic.

The grulla was ready to go to war now. He knew he was next, and I guess he'd liked this idea of idling around with a cold-running stream and a rick of hay close to hand whenever he wanted either. He planted his muzzle close to the dust and slipped behind a threesome of tall mules where maybe he thought I couldn't reach him.

There wasn't any way I was going to be outsmarted by some ignorant pony, though. I stepped sideways while his head was low and he couldn't see me. As soon as his head started to come up I snaked a loop past the rump of the last mule and got a clean head catch with the first throw.

The grulla squawled and backed, and that

rope was drawn up against the tail of the mule. Judging from the reaction, that particular animal was sensitive in that particular spot, and for a minute or so we had a penful of very active mules. When they settled down, though, I still had a whole rope, with me on the one end and the grulla on the other.

I was damned if I was going to give him the satisfaction of walking up to him by that time and so convinced him to do the walking over to me. By then Chic was saddled and ready to go.

I got my saddle on without the grulla getting out from under the blanket more than twice and cinched him up as if I was trying to cut him into thirds, flank cinch and all, as I had a good idea of what was coming and wanted a solid foundation. Even at that, the beast was trying to puff air on me, so I planted a knee in his belly and lashed my hull down all over again.

By this time he had such a hump in his back I was afraid his tail might get to tickling his nose and give him a sneezing fit. And I sure knew better than to tie our sacks of eatables in place just yet.

I slipped the bridle on and buckled it secure and put my rope where it belonged. Nor was I too proud to take what other advantage that I could, so I distracted him with a thorough ear-wringing while I stepped up and found my seat.

Right there inside the pen then, I turned loose of his ear and let him work out who was going to be the boss this day.

He was purely willing to take his turn at leadership. He threw his head to the left and almost got the job done by immediately darting away to the right, just the direction you might expect him to *not* go. If I hadn't had a good, solid hold on the horn he just might have had me flapping my arms and praying for feathers. As it happened, though, this was no fancy exhibition for the ladies and the swells but a serious argument between me and him, so I did have a hearty hold on the apple and would have tied on a bucking roll too had I thought of it ahead of time.

Still, what counted was that I was up there hanging on with hands, knees, and spurs when he was done with the move. I felt so good I let out a whoop and raked the grulla's shoulders with my rowels to encourage another leap. I got it, up and over, and raked him again.

I think the grulla was enjoying it then as much as I was. He leaped and twisted and tried to shake us both apart. He went into a fit of stiff-legged bouncing that would have rattled my head if there'd been anything in there. He tried a sudden squat to loosen my seat and ducked off to the side again. For some reason that particular thing has always been harder for me to sit than anything else, but it didn't work for him this time.

All in all we had us a fine old time and every so often made it that much more interesting by crashing into a mule or several and setting them off again. We might have kept it up a deal longer except that the man who owned the pen came by and hollered at me for disturbing his other customers, and so I sawed at the reins and hauled the grulla's head around until he got the idea we should quit fooling around and go do some work for a change. He was willing enough by then but could still take pride in his side of the scrap. I suspect I was smiling pretty broad when finally we left the pen and I swung down to load the rest of my stuff and join Chic.

CHAPTER 19

The horses we were to deliver turned out to be the kind that would bring out the greed in a churchgoing man.

There were five of them, each sleek and glossy with good health seeping out by way of shiny skin oils. Full bodied and heavy muscled without being the least bit fat. Strong, well-made heads with wide nostrils just made for gathering in the wind on a long run. Their chests were wide and deep showing plenty of lung. They had decently built rumps, though not with the thick muscle pads of sprinters. Rather they had the long, full, smoothly muscled forequarters of distance horses. And the short, barely curved back that indicates strength in that area.

One look and you could see that these were five-hundred-dollar horses, and it was no wonder that their owner would pay handsomely to have animals like these protected and tended and watched over during delivery.

Nor was it any wonder that the seller — I assumed him to be the seller, although he never said — would not have been so trusted. In fact, I wondered how such a man would ever have come into possession of such fine horseflesh.

Somehow this man reminded me much of a water rat. Scraggly and patchy and pointy-faced, his clothes and his person were both ill-kept and unpleasant. Don't get me wrong now. I'm not some kind of swell who expects a man to smell of lavender water like a fancy-house lady. I've spent a power of time working out where the baths come maybe once at each change of season. A man can get to smelling pretty ripe at a time like that. But that isn't what I mean at all. That is just a matter of being dirty. This man was filthy in a whole different way. And I guess what it boils down to is that I didn't like him when I saw him and never found a reason to change my opinion later.

Those horses, though. Now they were something.

When we first saw them they were lazing comfortably in a ramshackle corral thrown together of scraps and limbs and apparently whatever had wanted to fall off a convenient tree. Those animals had a quality about them, though, that brought the place to life and made it a thing of beauty set back there at the end of a long, narrow, deeply shaded gorge in what must have been a gold-free part of the hills if you could judge by the lack of miners and mining activity.

At that first look they were just standing in a bare corral, but these were no hang-head, hip-shot, undernourished ponies. They'd heard us coming, of course, and all five heads were proudly erect, all five sets of ears cocked alertly toward us, all five pairs of nostrils flared to catch the scents that would've been drifting upcanyon. Their eyes were wide and clear and seeking. They had what I've heard other men describe as "the look of eagles" about them.

We entered the yard between the corral and the poorly built shanty near it, and Chic swung down without waiting for an invitation. Although it was not a thing I would normally do, I stepped down immediately as well and walked to the rails where I could more clearly admire those animals.

Behind me Chic called out a firm, "Howdy," and I remembered my manners in time to turn and join him as the man who had the horses walked out into what little light there was here.

"You'd be York?" Chic asked.

"And if I am?"

"Then I'd tell you a word, and Bert an' me would ride off with them horses."

"Tell me the word then, boy."

"Tell me your name an' I will," Chic said, which was not like him at all.

"York," the man said.

"An' you'd know who gave me the word?" Chic prodded.

York nodded. "Ollie Mantus," he said.

"All right. He said to tell you 'payday,' " Chic said.

Again York nodded. He squinted up at the sky — what could be seen of it from the bottom of this long, skinny pit — and grudgingly said, "Comin' late, I reckon. I s'pose you'll have to stay over." Such a cheerful, willing invitation I've scarcely had before. You bet.

Chic gave him our names and agreeably said, "We'll get our gear an' bring it in."

I wasn't especially anxious to stay the night here. For one thing, these high, close walls made me nervous in a way that the rock and hills above Deadwood did not. But I was not about to do anything that would queer me getting hold of those horses for however short a time.

We stripped the gear from our animals,

and I led them into the corral while Chic toted stuff into the shack.

I'd really been coming to like my grulla, but in company like this he looked scruffy and kind of puny. I mean, he was a nice enough range pony, but when you put a fifty-dollars-tops horse in with something like these, well, there's not much you can say. I stood there for a few minutes longer just looking before I joined Chic and York inside.

York's home, if that is what it was, was not even on a level with a two-bit spread's line camps.

It was made of vertically set poles that had been indifferently chinked with clay mud. Whoever had dug the floor hadn't bothered to dig it square or even smooth so it was full of miniature escarpments and mountain ranges. Enough protruding rocks were left in their natural, undisturbed state to discourage even the most callous-footed night walker from leaving his boots under the bunk.

Of bunks there were four, one pegged into each corner with a single leg for each and the rest of the support coming from the wall pegs. A mud-and-rock fireplace was built into the back wall. Shelves on that wall held some sacks of dry foods and things. A few pegs in the front wall held hangables. And that was all there was to the furnishings. No table. No chairs. The bunk edges had to serve for all that. And as it turned out, the bunks were not so much as sprung with crossed ropes. They were built of poles closely laid from end to end and covered with awfully skinny straw-and-burlap mattresses. The floor probably would've been better except for the rocks that made it worse.

York had a dirty iron pot and an even dirtier iron spider on the floor in front of the fireplace. The pot held some suspicious-looking remains.

"I'll have our dinner ready directly," the man said. He slopped some water from a bucket in on top of the old stuff in the pot, took a sack from one of the shelves and spilled in some dried beans. A few sticks of jerked meat into the pot and a handful of desiccated onion and he seemed to figure he'd done his duty as a cook and a host. He set the pot into the fire where it could fend for itself until he chose to serve the meal.

In fairness I would have to say that I don't really believe he was showing any meanness toward us there. I suspect he'd have had the same for his supper had he been alone. The only change would likely have been in the amount he cooked.

I felt a need to visit the privy and asked the way. York hooked a casual thumb toward the doorway. "Outside," he said. "G'wan downstream, huh?"

I quickly discovered what he meant. There wasn't anything so fancy as a formal, set-aside privy area, just whatever looked comfortable. In a way I was surprised he'd bothered to suggest I go downstream from the shack.

When I got back inside he and Chic were sitting on the one blanket-covered bunk. From some hidden corner, York had produced a jug. I joined them and discovered that this, at least, was all right. I took a pull at it and felt nicely warmed all the way down.

"You'll make it easy in two days," York was saying. "Ollie gave you extra time just to cover his bets, like. He's like that, Ollie is. Always thinking ahead, see? Always plans things out. Leaves room for things to go wrong, like. He's a good boy, Ollie. I've been knowin' him a long time."

"We won't have any trouble," Chic said.

"Nah," York agreed. "Not with Ollie planning things, you won't. Just listen to what he says an' do it that way an' you won't have any problems. His daddy was like that too.

Yard wide and a mile long, either one of them. Trust anything they say. I been doing that a long time, see? Take my word for it, boy. I know."

Anything that might encourage Chic and me to be just like York was not exactly my idea of a recommendation, but of course I did not say so.

York cocked a bright, rat's eye and looked shrewdly from Chic to me and back to Chic. "I've an idea you'll see what I mean if you have sense enough to be patient, see? Just keep your mouths shut an' pay attention. You'll do all right."

"It sounds like you've been angling for a permanent job, Chic," I put in. I was surprised but pleased too.

"We'll see how it goes," Chic said. "See if we like the work." There was a mixture of both hope and doubt in his voice. Whatever, it didn't last long. He reached for the jug and took a long, belly burner of a swallow and passed it back to York.

"Good stuff, huh?" York asked conversationally. He couldn't have expected any disagreement from us. "You don't hafta be shy, boys. Drink up. We got a bunch of this from a freighter on the Cheyenne to Deadwood road, see? Got most of a barrel here in this gulch an' two more tucked into a hole in the ground out closer to the road." He took a deep pull following his own advice and sighed. "Sure is better'n trade whiskey." One got the idea York was well acquainted with trade whiskey too.

"Does this, uh, Ollie raise his own horses?" I asked. I didn't figure he did or we wouldn't be delivering them, but I wanted to get the talk around to those animals and any mention of this Ollie person — I'd forgotten his last name for the moment — seemed the likeliest way to get York to open up. After all, I like my whiskey, but I'd rather drink it than talk about it. For talking purposes, I'll take horses any old time.

"Nah," York scoffed. "Ollie's too smart to be tied down that way, he is. But he sure as hell can pick 'em, can't he? Went all the way out to Kentucky for these. They traced the bloodlines away back, he said. Thorough-bred sires. The dams are half Morgan an' half quarter-running horses, that on the mare line." He shook his head in admiration. "Ollie sure knows horses, he does."

I agreed. He did know his horses. And I sure tucked away that knowledge of the breeding combination that had led to those animals out in York's rickety corral. It was a thing I wanted to duplicate someday. If they had any cow sense tucked into those pretty heads, they would be well-nigh perfect. The kind of animal a man could make a fine living from, raising those and nothing else.

York passed the jug one more time and stood with the cautious motion of one in whose bones rheumatism is starting to build. "Supper oughta be ready, boys. Find you a plate if you wanta eat. Set still and go hongry if you'd ruther."

Given that choice I wasn't at all sure which would be the better, but I got a plate anyway. I'm still not sure which would have been the better choice.

CHAPTER 20

Those horses were broken out to handle as nice as they looked. We tied them in tandem on one long lead in the army manner so that one person with the end of that one lead rope had control of the whole string.

And I would have to admit that we weren't five miles down the road before I called a halt to the procession.

"What's the matter, Bert?"

"Something I just gotta do is what." I dropped out of the saddle and began tugging loose my cinch straps.

"Dammit, Bert, are you doin' what I think you're doin'?"

I grinned at him and said, "Uh huh. Surest thing you know, I am."

"Bert, now you shouldn't ought t' do that. I don't think Ollie'd like it."

"Aw, hell, Chic. When did you turn into a mother hen? Why I've seen you do pure craziness just so you could laugh into the wind, old friend. And this isn't craziness. I just gotta ride one of these animals or I'll bust from fretting over it. And it's not like there'd be any harm done. Chic, I just *got* to feel one of these devils under me."

He shook his head and rubbed at the back of his neck some, but he smiled — I think maybe he was remembering some of the fun we'd had together back at the OX5 — and got down to help me with the horse holding.

I peeled the tail-end horse off the string and shifted my gear to his back, replacing him on the lead with my grulla. The grulla didn't necessarily like being there, but he wasn't going to get into too much trouble back there at the end of the line. For one thing, a cow horse like him was used to the idea of ropes. For another, even if he wanted to raise some hell, he wasn't going to be dragging four heavier animals along with him regardless. Chic took over the lead string while I got acquainted with my new mount.

Well, I stepped onto him and would you believe it? It was kind of disappointing. Oh, he was some well-trained horse. He never offered to bite or buck or even to ask politely which of us was to be the boss. The horse stood and waited while I got myself comfortable. I didn't have to fling myself into some quick but cling-tight seat before I might come unglued. He waited patiently for instruction and then did exactly what was asked of him — but no more than that. After five miles or so I said, the hell with it and switched my saddle back to my own grulla. Chic never said a word, though he did smile a little as if to himself.

We made it comfortably to where we were supposed to be by evening of the second day out of York's place. Chic found it by what must have been an awfully complicated and powerfully detailed set of directions, for as far as I could tell we were tucked in at the base of just another one of the many abrupt, grass-sloped buttes rising out of this broad and beautiful short-grass country.

We unsaddled, threw our gear into a protected little fold of rock above a tiny seep at the foot of the butte, and were home for as long as we chose to be.

The horses, both our own and Ollie's, we hobbled and turned loose to fill up on that marvelous, rich grass. They could come up whenever they wished as well to drink from the slight overflow of the little seep. There was enough of it to satisfy the needs of so few animals.

I liked the place. There was no way a cow-loving waddie such as me could not like it, for it was perfect country for the raising of beef and was as yet ungrazed. If any meat was being made here now, it was wild meat, and the sight of such perfect grazing lands going unused was enough to put ideas into my pointy little head. Especially after admiring those horses for the past couple days.

Somebody was sure to be bringing beef in here soon. Men who'd seen this country as they passed through toward the Black Hills wouldn't stay gold crazy forever. As soon as the Indians were brought under control, those men would be remembering.

And if another man had himself a start on a horse herd by then . . . well . . . there was no telling what could be built or where the idea could be taken. This spot right here . . . I could just see a tight little house built snug in the protection of the butte. The seep proved there was water to be had. Corrals, maybe even a hay barn could be put in the lee of the butte. And maybe there could be a place for a girl named Elaine in that house. Oh, it was a grand idea and one I thoroughly enjoyed while we waited.

And while we waited I tried to learn more from Chic about our employer and the prospects we might have for a good job.

"He's a big man around here, Bert, an' he

might could get us some . . ."

"Easy money?"

He shook his head so hard it practically vibrated. "No, it's . . . quick money maybe. You couldn't hardly call it easy."

The next day I found out what he meant.

The next day Oliver Mantus and four of his riders came fogging around the north end of our pleasant butte, and I quickly learned what Chic had been talking about. And what he'd tried to avoid talking about.

Mantus was a short, thick-bodied, powerfully built man of forty or so, with a spare beard and wind-tangled, overlong hair. He was dressed in rough clothes and carried a brace of revolvers strapped around the outside of his coat. That would have been a dumb-seeming thing to do except that it made him look so awful mean that you knew without having to think about it that this was just the effect he wanted. And got.

The other four were just as tough-looking, and two of them had short-barreled shotguns slung on their saddles. All five were heavily armed.

Altogether I would have to say that these were not people I wanted to work either with or for.

"You're right on time, Ollie," Chic said by

way of a greeting.

Mantus gave him a toothy smile that fell some short of reaching his eyes. "It's a good policy, Robertson. You might want to remember that." He gave me a brief, raking glance and a curt nod.

All five men were off their horses and pulling saddles practically before their sweating horses were stopped. I was surprised to see that these horses, heaving from a hard run, were of poor quality. Twenty-dollar mounts if they were worth that much.

Chic motioned me to follow and hurried to catch the hobbled fresh horses and lead them to Mantus and his men. When they were all close to hand, Chic asked Mantus, "Is anyone behind you?"

This time Mantus's quick, answering smile looked positively vicious. "You can count on it, Robertson. In this business it isn't a question of 'if,' it's a matter of 'when.' And we don't wait long enough to answer that one. It's hit 'n git, as the man says, and the devil take the hindmost."

Mantus flopped his saddle onto the fresh, fine horse and cinched it tight. He transferred his bridle to it and stepped back toward the ill-bred and ill-used horse he'd been riding. Without a pause he pulled a revolver from his belt and dropped the dun gelding with a well-placed bullet to the brain. Within a minute or so the others had done the same. The sight of those five twitching and, as far as I could see, totally needless carcasses damn near made me sick. It fouled the sight of that beautiful grass country for me, and the dream-visions I'd been having were blown out of my head along with those shots.

"No fuss and no follow-up, you see, Robertson? And no way they can use a dead horse as a spare to push on after us." He took a small sack from his coat pocket. "Are your horses watered, Robertson?"

"Sure. Just like you said."

Mantus nodded. He seemed satisfied by the answer. "See that they don't drink out of this seep again then. It will clear in about a week, but I wouldn't recommend using it before then." He stepped to the seep and spilled a flow of white crystals into the water. The sack he carefully folded and replaced into his pocket even though it was empty.

He must have seen my questioning look, for he smiled. It was almost a normal and natural expression this time. "Poison," he told me in a matter-of-fact way. "It wouldn't do for the posse to spot this bag and get suspicious. More likelihood of dismounting some of them this way. All of them if we're lucky."

Never a thought, it seemed, to all the other animals that might drink that water in the next week. People, too, for that matter. He hadn't said anything about people, but I sure never heard of a poison that would take a horse but not a man. Sure most people would drink from the flow, but you couldn't count on that. Again it seemed a cruel and a needless thing for the man to do.

"We'll be going now," he said, this time directing it to the both of us and not just to Chic. "It's up to you, but I would suggest you do the same."

Mantus reached into another pocket and drew out a clinking handful of coins. He handed them to Chic. "You'll find a little bonus here for you and your partner, Robertson. You boys did all right." He slapped Chic on the shoulder. "If you are interested, drop around at Hobarth's roadhouse in about a week's time. We might work out something to your advantage and to mine."

Chic took the money and stared at the yellow coins nested in his palm. He seemed almost under a spell to them for a moment. He brought himself back from wherever he'd been and asked, "Hobarth's? Where would that be?"

Mantus laughed. "You can find it if you look in the right places. Call that a test if you like."

In another minute they were gone. Chic and I were alone on the empty grass with two live horses, five dead ones, and a poisoned water hole. Lord God, but I felt awful just then.

CHAPTER 21

"Tell me about it," I said.

Chic was wearing a genuine hangdog expression, as he had every right to do under the circumstances. He walked slowly toward where our horses were grazing, and I matched him step for step. He was right to do that, of course. It wouldn't do for our own animals to get into the water Mantus had just finished tainting.

"Well," Chic said finally, "you remember I was in that game back at Deadwood."

"Uh huh."

"Yeah, well, I sorta lost more than we had." He looked at me closely. "I had what shoulda been a sure thing, Bert. That's the only way it happened, I swear."

I nodded. It didn't really make any difference now anyway.

"So anyhow, I lost what I had an' owed some more, and Ollie . . . he was in the game then . . . he said he'd cover the debt for me if I'd go an' have a drink in his room an' consider workin' for him to pay it off. Hell, it sounded simple enough, an' I knew you was ready to get back to work anyways, so I said all right."

He sighed deeply. "It turned out that Ollie knew all about that mixup with the hardrock miner. What was his name? Loomis?"

"Uh huh. Morgan Loomis." I wasn't about to forget that. And maybe Chic had just as much reason not to remember it.

"Yeah. Morgan Loomis. Anyway, Ollie knew all about that. I guess he'd known it right along. If we can believe what he says, he's the reason no one called us on it while we were messin' around in Deadwood there.

"So Ollie said he needed a good hand or two t' help set up this horse switch after him an' his boys hit a shipment of some kind . . . gold, I s'pect . . . between Deadwood and Cheyenne. He said he'd forget what I owed him an' pay us a hundred dollars over that. An' he said it could work into somethin' better afterward. Which is what he meant by askin' us to meet him at this Hobarth's place. I guess we c'n join up with him if we want."

"Yeah," I said, just as nasty as I could make one word sound.

"Aw hell, Bert. You know I never meant for us t' go join him or anything. I just figured we could lead the fresh horses down here an' hand 'em over to him an' be done with it. That's all. An' that's all we done, too. We just delivered five head of horses, Bert. We never robbed whatever it is those boys robbed nor we hadn't a hand in it. We can just get on out o' this country an' be shut of the whole thing. The way you been wanting to do anyhow."

Ponder it as I might, there just was not a lot I could say to Chic that would accomplish a thing, and there was nothing either of us could say or do that would change any of it. What I did do was lead the grulla back to where my gear was lying. "Let's get out of here," I said.

We headed southeast. I'd heard there were some stock cows being moved onto grass down in Nebraska, and right then I did not give much of a fat, flying flap if we ran into any of the Indians who were supposed to be so stirred up by people moving into the hills. In the first place I hadn't seen any such Indians and did not much put stock in the scare stories about them. And secondly, if any of them *did* want to complain to us about what other people were doing here, it would be tough luck on the Indians, the mood I was in right then. So we rode until we found a place with clean, untainted water and stopped there for the night.

In the morning we pushed southeast again. We hadn't gone more than a mile when Chic clucked to get my attention.

"Yeah?"

He pointed. A group of riders was coming over a rise behind us, moving at a hard gallop as if they had every intention of catching up to us in a hurry. There turned out to be five of them when they were all on the near side of the rise.

"It doesn't look like Mantus's crowd," I said.

"I'm afraid not."

"Trouble?"

"Likely."

"What do we do now?"

"Oh, God, Bert, I jus' don't know." He took a deep breath. And he checked to see that his revolver was loose in the holster.

I suppose I should have felt worse about that possibility, but the truth is that I did not. It was beginning to look like our backs were up against it, between that quick-triggered Loomis and that miserable Oliver Mantus, but if it came to that then it just did, and we'd do what we had to do. It would depend on who these people were and whether they were willing to listen to another side of it all. And so I checked my revolver too to make sure the caps were in place and it was ready to go.

We drew rein right where we were and turned to wait for them to catch up to us. We never tried to run or to hide, and I would swear any oath that Chic was as willing as me to talk to these boys before we did anything else.

We waited and they came on and as soon as they saw we were aware of them, the one in front turned and did some motioning to the others. He was probably telling them what to do, but we were too far away to hear. They reined wide apart and spread out into a fan as they swept toward us. I didn't like that.

I did what little I could to ease their minds. I took my right hand away from my gun and lifted my hat and waved them in. It did no good.

As they got close they brought out their guns and leveled them, and the one who'd been riding in front let fly with a bullet before they were really within good short-gun range.

They fired first, and I would swear any oath on that subject too. They didn't have to do that, but they did.

The others opened up too, and I heard a bullet thump into the ground nearby and whine away to the rear. That was the only bullet I heard through the whole, brief thing. But then they were on moving horses and we were sitting still. Their aim could not have been too easy.

Chic's gun was already out and working, and almost right away I saw a man tumble out of the saddle. He landed so limp and loose that he looked for sure like he was gone.

I put my hat back on my head and pulled my revolver free. The odd thing about it was that I was feeling completely calm and unhurried about it all. I didn't even feel afraid of being hit and took my time with what I had to do.

I cocked the revolver and brought the sights down on the nearest rider and went to squeeze the trigger and could not, and that was all right too. I found that I did not mind that a bit. It was merely a useful and interesting piece of information but not one that seemed important or especially worrisome. In no hurry at all, I changed my aim to the horse the man was riding and made a picture-pretty chest shot that dropped the animal and sent its rider sprawling into the grass. I took time to note that he'd dropped his gun and seemed too shaken to care.

They were close now, the two riders that were left. That meant Chic had already spilled two of them, I decided. I tipped my elderly revolver to the side to let the spent cap fall free of the mechanism while I recocked it and then shot another horse. The rider of that one landed very heavily, and I remember hoping he had not hurt himself.

Everything looked very clear at the time, colors very bright and every line and shading very sharply defined.

I saw a splash of dust square on the chest of the last rider, and the man slid out of his saddle. He, too, landed with the finality of a flour sack being dropped onto a hard floor.

"C'mon, Bert. I'm empty."

I looked at Chic. He was hauling his yellow horse around and already hooking him with his spurs.

Chic's words were the first sounds I remember hearing after hearing the whine of that one bullet.

I spun the grulla and raked him and kited off after Chic, who was already racing up the side of the low hill we'd been about to climb when those men came onto us. I heard a gun, maybe more, fire behind me. I raked the grulla again and pushed him all the harder for the safety of that hilltop.

The grulla scrambled belly-down across the top and damn near ran into Chic, who had pulled up there. We got things under control again and Chic leaped down to the ground. He threw the yellow's reins to me and hollored, "Wait here!" He ran back the way we'd just come, dropping to his belly and crawling the last little way.

It seemed a long time until he came back. When he did he looked worried.

"There's three of them still alive," he said. "One hit it looks like but not too bad. Two horses." He shook his head. "That's damn tough luck, Bert. They seen us good. They got close enough to see us awful good." He felt of his gun butt, and I knew what he was thinking.

"No, Chic," I said, and I guess I said it pretty sharply for he looked a bit startled. "We leave those men alone now, hear? Far as they know it's us who's in the wrong. They won't be following us with one man hurt and a horse short. And we leave them alone."

"But —"

"No! I know what you're figuring. They'll go back to the hills or even down to Cheyenne, and they'll tell it around, and we'll be wanted. Well, all right. If that's it, then that's it. But we will *not* go to murdering people.

We just aren't going to start that. Not for any reason."

"Elaine might hear of it," he said.

I stared back at him without saying a word. I hoped I didn't need to.

Again he ran his fingertips over the gun butt. When he looked up again though, I could see in his eyes that he wasn't going to push me on this. "All right, Bert. But I *sure* hope you know what you're doin' here." He retrieved his reins and got back onto the yellow. "Nebraska still?"

I grinned. "Texas maybe. Or Mexico even. How're you with talking Mexican?"

"Give me a choice between that an' hanging an' I bet I can learn it just fine."

"Good, 'cause that could be the choice we have. I've got some friends down south who can tell us which way the wind is blowing down home. They'll give us the nod if it's safe to stay. Otherwise we'll keep going."

Chic nodded. He started forward but stopped the yellow horse. "Bert?"

"Uh huh?"

"I'm sorry about this, Bert."

"I know." And I meant it. I knew he really did regret what we'd gotten into. In a way you could put the blame on him for putting us here, but in another way it was just one of those mean, stupid, unlucky things that can happen to people, and that was the way I preferred to look at it. Especially since there was no way to change any of it now. It was way too late for that. "Come on," I said. "We've got little enough time until those boys get back to a telegraph line. We better not waste any of what we have."

We rode on then and made it a full mile before Chic reined over beside me and plucked weakly at my wrist. He was pasty pale. "Let's stop a minute, huh?"

"Sure." I helped him down off the yellow. He was shaking so hard he couldn't have managed by himself without falling. When I let go of him he slumped the rest of the way down until he was sitting half huddled over on the ground. "You'll be all right in a minute," I told him for lack of anything better to say.

The best response he could get out was a slight nodding that was scarcely noticeable amid the shaking. It was quite a while before we could go on.

CHAPTER 22

Whatever Mantus and his boys had decided to rob, they had sure gone to throwing rocks at hornets' nests when they did it. A body would think we could count on a fair amount of time — say a couple days or so — before the word could get around on what had happened and who to be looking for. Not so.

Within a matter of a few lousy hours, I was beginning to think that Chic and I might be the only people in the whole of that country who didn't know what Mantus had done. We pushed our horses slow but steady well into the night, grabbed a few hours' sleep, and got started again well before first light. It was only that extra-early start that kept us from maybe having more trouble that quick again.

Just before dawn we were plodding around the west side of one of those grassy buttes, of which we were beginning to see fewer as we went south. As we neared the far end of the mound we caught the faint, distant sounds of men talking.

Both of us pulled up, and Chic gave me a quick, harried look. There should have been no one anywhere around here.

"I'll take a look," Chic whispered.

I nodded and reached to hold his horse.

Chic stroked the butt of his revolver and resettled his hat nervously before he cat-footed forward. It seemed an empty country once he disappeared around a bulge in the slope we were skirting.

I edged the horses in tighter to the slope to cut down on the chance of anyone seeing them. The air was moistly cool at this hour and very still. For some reason that made it seem all the more lonesome.

The animals sure showed no sign of discomfort at the delay. We hadn't been going long this morning, but we had worked them late that night before and they'd come up a little short on their rest and grazing time in between. They stood with their heads hanging and with not the least hint of fidgeting or stamping. My grulla at least shifted from hip to hip. The yellow didn't even do that.

Had I dared I would have slid down to the ground and loosened their cinches, but there was no telling what might be going on down at the end of the butte — which I was trying not to dwell on in my own imagination. One thing I knew for sure. If I heard shots from down that way, those horses and I had to be ready to go and right now. If Chic needed help, he'd need it now, not when I might get done fiddling with cinches.

Before I had time to draw too many mind-pictures of the things Chic might be facing down there he came back into sight. He was hurrying along at a half-running pace.

"It's another posse, Bert," he said raggedly when he was beside me. He was breathing pretty hard, so it must have been further than I'd guessed.

"You're sure?"

He gave me a dirty look. "Well I didn't walk up to 'em and *ask*, for cryin' out loud." He swung into the saddle and shook his head. "If they aren't a posse, I don't know what they would be. You never saw so many guns. Big ones, little ones, a bunch of 'em carrying shotguns. I didn't count, but there must be a dozen men in the group. Every one of 'em actin' like he was taking a holiday. Laughing and scratching and having a fine time. They're a posse, all right. I seen the like before once, though from the other side of the table to what we're on now."

Yes, and I had too and hadn't seen a thing wrong with it at the time. It sure had a different look from over here.

"Can we slip around them?" I asked.

"We can do anything if we're lucky enough, but I wouldn't count on bein' that lucky. There's nothin' but short grass to block their view for miles to the south an' to either side. 'Bout all we can do is turn back north and hope they don't think to climb this hill until we're well gone. Go north an' then east maybe. See if we can get around without runnin' into these boys or others like them."

He resettled his hat again and arranged the reins between his fingers. "I sure wish I knew where Mantus got to," he said. "Knowin' that sly bastard had himself a hidey-hole picked out ahead of time an' a way to get there. If I knew where it was, we'd sure run to it right along with him."

"Maybe it's just as well we don't know then," I said, which drew an odd look from my friend. "Let's go on out of here, then, before they start getting restless and go a-wandering."

Which is what we did. We turned our horses back north and began wasting those miles we'd earned this morning and during the night.

You know, I have heard it said that in rolling country like this, where it looks like you can see for ten miles in any direction, a tribe of Indians can pass within a couple hundred yards of a crack cavalry outfit and never be seen, just by taking advantage of the low points in the ground. For all I know, this could be quite true. But I sure felt barenaked for a long time there and was not willing to test the idea, with my neck and Chic's the table stakes we stood to lose for being wrong.

So we rode north for several hours and found ourselves an east-west running chain of smooth-sided buttes to get behind before we were willing to turn east. We didn't know what that posse might be doing to the south of us, and it was entirely possible that they might've chanced to ride north too.

We pushed on until noon and — the fact is — were too downright scared to build a fire and so went without a midday meal. All we had with us in the way of eatables was dried beans and a dough-ball mixture of flour and salt and powder to which we could add water, but either one had to be cooked or it wasn't worth throwing away.

We stopped for a noon rest anyway as it

would not do to overtax the horses. There was no way we could know when we might have to ask them for a hard run and so we had to keep them as fit as prolonged use would allow. They were still fresh enough now, but if we wasted them early it could go hard with us later.

Chic climbed to the top of a small, set-apart hill, too low and rounded to really be called a butte, and signaled there was no one in sight, so I went ahead and hobbled both horses, pulled the bridles, and slipped their cinches loose. That was about the best we could do for them. When I was done I climbed up to join him.

"Big country, isn't it?" I observed after I'd flopped to the ground beside him.

"Too damn big or not big enough, I cain't decide," he said.

I knew what he meant. Maybe too big for us to get out of. Maybe not big enough to hide in.

From where we sat on the hard, stony ground, you could see in all directions for a couple hours' ride, more than an hour even at a horse-killing run, so for the moment we were safe enough while we sat and watched the horses pick at the short clumps of bunch grass that covered this country. Again I could not help thinking how well cattle would do here. As it was, there was nothing in our view but ourselves and our horses and, far off, a hawk circling slowly while he waited for a rabbit or a mouse to show itself.

We were there more than an hour and were beginning to feel a lot more relaxed when Chic reached over and punched my arm. "Dust," he said.

I sighed. He was right. Something was moving off to the west of us. "Time to go," I agreed. We slipped back away from the hilltop and hurried down the slope, moving faster than maybe we needed to but unable to slow down no matter how foolish we knew ourselves to be. We might know there was no need for haste at this point, but we couldn't feel that knowledge and so we hurried like so many mice scurrying aside from that stooping hawk.

And that was the way it went for the next six days. Every direction we turned, we found someone there. Every time we rested we saw someone's dust moving up on us. Every time we slept we did it in fear of what we would see on waking.

Once we made it nearly as far south as the UP tracks, but a party of riders coursing back and forth and seemingly looking for sign, turned us back yet again. In the end, out of food now and with our horses gaunted from too much travel and too little rest, we turned back into the Black Hills in search of a refuge. We headed toward York's shack as being the only shelter we knew of where we might be welcomed without first being shot.

Under the circumstances, getting back to that miserable shack was damn near like coming home. We climbed off our horses gratefully and turned them loose into York's pen. They hadn't been too much time lately with their backs bare, and they got down and rolled first thing. It looked so good I was tempted to join them.

York was not at home but his food was, and we were proud to discover that he'd done some store shopping while we were away. There was a huge tin of ready-baked crackers on the shelf and we dug into those while we waited for a pot of beans and onions and jerked meat to boil. When finally it did, I was so hungry I didn't even mind the nasty condition of that iron pot. We each grabbed spoons and dipped them straight into the pot without worrying about such niceties as plates or bowls. Before long we began to feel almost human again. We let the fire die off and crawled onto York's hard, lousy, wonderful bunks. But we kept our guns close to hand.

York came floating in the next day. If he was surprised to see us, he didn't say so. As a matter of fact, he came inside with no more than a brief nod and looked around the place before he spoke at all. "You've eat a couple dollars' worth of food, I see," was the first thing he said to us.

Chic took the hint and dug out a half eagle for him.

York grunted and asked, "D'Ollie get his horses all right?"

Chic shrugged.

"He was fine when he left us," I said, "and we've no reason to think any different now. If he'd taken us with him or told us what to expect, we'd have been a lot better off between then and now."

Chic gave me something of a dirty look — maybe I wasn't ever supposed to question the great man's judgment — but York cackled out loud.

"That Ollie's a smart one, didn't I tell you? If anybody's gonna be trailed, it ain't gonna be him, see? Oh, I like that boy. Smart as they come, he is."

"Pretty damn hard on us, though," I protested in spite of Chic.

York took no offense from it. "Ain't that the truth," he said with delight. He thumped on his knee some and shook his head in admiration for that brilliant planner, Oliver Mantus.

Hell, there was no point in me trying to complain about it now anyway. If only because York's hide was too thick and too dirt-crusted to get a needle through to where he'd feel it, there wasn't. Besides which, if he ever did realize that I wasn't too happy with his boss he might turn the both of us out of here, and we had no place else to go. So I shut up.

"The question is," Chic put in when he'd decided I was going to sit still and be good again, "where do Bert 'n me go from here? We can't hole up here with you forever, I reckon."

York scratched himself and grinned. "Not no longer'n your money holds out, you can't. Till then you can make yourselves welcome, though."

"That ain't exactly my notion o' heaven," Chic said.

York shrugged and never lost his grin. "Suit yourselves, boys," he said. "It's all the same to me."

Chic looked thoughtful for a moment and mused, "I don't s'pose you've ever heard of a place called . . . what was it now? . . . Hobarth's? Yeah, that's it. I don't suppose you'd know where we could find this Hobarth's roadhouse?"

All the mirth was gone from York's face as quick as the name was spoken. Of a sudden this grimy old man was cold-eyed and cautious, and I began to realize that there might have been a time when men would've stepped out of his path when he walked.

"Where'd you get that name?" he demanded.

Chic must've seen the change that had come over York, but he sure never gave any sign of it. Still loose and casual he said, "Ollie mentioned it to us. He said we might wanta stop by and see him there. Talk some business. Like that, it was."

Again the change was both overwhelming and instantaneous. From a suspicious retreat, York's expression leaped to one of open pleasure. He jumped to his feet and pounded both of us on the shoulders. "By damn, boys, I thought you to be right ones when I first saw you. Yessir, I did for a fact." He hustled across the lumpy floor at such a rapid, foot-dragging pace that he raised a dust from the dry dirt amid the stones. When he came back he had another jug in his hands.

He hefted the jug and sloshed it near his ear once. "Hell, boys, I knew you for honest ones too. You ain't even been into this while

259

I was away. Yessir, that Ollie sure knows how to pick them. Have a drink on Ollie, boys. What belongs to him now you can use too, I reckon." He pulled the cob stopper and had a healthy swallow for himself before he handed us the jug.

I noticed he did not offer to return Chic's five dollars for the food we had eaten.

Not that I was thinking so much about that just then anyway. It seemed that somehow Chic and I had gone and joined a bunch of robbers and Lord knows what else. And without even knowing it at the time.

CHAPTER 23

Hobarth's wasn't far removed in appearance from York's shack except there was more of it. A regular collection of shacks both big and little.

Mantus had called it a roadhouse, but the only way it could be considered such would be because the biggest shack was an open, one-room affair where a man could get a drink or find a card game or stock up from the barrels of dried foods placed off in one corner. The whole affair was way the hell and gone away from any road.

It was up in the northwest corner of the hills in some dry, rough country that hadn't yet caught the eye of any passing gold-seekers. Or maybe those that did come this far were discouraged from staying. I wouldn't know about that.

Chic and I had found the place from directions and on horses provided by old York. As soon as he knew where we were going, he insisted on us waiting at his place long enough — a couple days it had turned out to be — for him to lead our horses off somewhere and swap them for something not so recognizable. What he had come back with were a leggy bay and a long-bodied chestnut. He even had bills of sale for them proving that I'd paid seventy-five dollars for the bay and, in a different hand and differ-ent ink, that Chic had bought the chestnut for fifteen dollars and one burro. Which proves something, I guess, about the value of a bill of sale.

Personally, I was ready to ride south again as soon as we were out of sight of York's place on those new horses, but Chic wouldn't hear of it.

"Come on now, Bert. We told Ollie we'd meet him at Hobarth's. An' we took these horses as a binder on our word, didn't we?"

"We did not. We never said aye, nay, or maybe about meeting Mantus later, and our animals were worth every bit as much as these. The way I see it, nobody is owing anybody here. And I'd sure rather head back to Texas than go up to that snake's nest York was telling us about."

"By God, Bert, you may've forgot about all the lawboys strung out between here an' there, but I haven't. The way for us to stay clear of 'em is to hole up at Hobarth's awhile till Ollie says things are clear again. An' it ain't like we *have* to take up with him if we don't want. Why, we c'n ride on any time we want after we've talked with the man. An' you know how generous he is. Didn' he give us twice what he'd promised just for carryin' those horses to him? That's nothing t' sneeze at, Bert. That's awful good pay for so little work."

"We damn near got ourselves killed for that little piece of work, Chic. What's damn near as bad is that some others *did* get themselves killed for it."

"We never did anything wrong," Chic insisted. "You know that as well as I do. We never done a thing but carry some horses to a man, an' we got paid for it better'n any pay we've ever had before. Now you cain't argue with that."

What I couldn't argue with was Chic. His mind was made up as firm as a good smith's weld, and there was no way I was going to change it. In the end we rode north by York's directions and found Hobarth's roadhouse with no trouble at all once we knew where to look.

We got there in the late afternoon and, not knowing what to expect, tied our horses at a rail in front of the public house rather than turning them in to the corral that was built close by.

There were only three customers in the place when we entered, but one of them was Mantus and another was a man who'd been riding with him for that robbery. All three were seated and leaning on the same corner table near the barrels that served as a bar.

When we went in Mantus got to his feet and held his hand out and made a show of welcoming us. "Robertson! Good to see you boys. We heard you had some trouble but came out of it. Didn't know but what you might have been hit, though, and the laws not know it. Good to see you, Robertson, an, uh . . ."

Chic made the introductions, and Mantus smiled. "Felloe, huh? Right. Good to see you here too, Fella." He turned toward a thin and very ordinary-looking man standing back by the barrels. "Two cups of the best for these boys, Jack. They will be welcome here any time from now on. Remember that, Jack."

Mantus dragged us back to his table and sat down and as soon as we had some whiskey — it tasted like the same stuff as we'd been drinking at York's — he pumped Chic for details of the fight we'd had with the posse. When Chic was done, Mantus wanted the selfsame story out of me.

"Good," he said when we were finished. "That's very good, boys. It shows you react well to the unexpected. That's very important, you know. Try as you might, you can never plan ahead for everything. You must always be prepared for the unexpected as well. That is one of the keys to success."

Mantus showed yellow teeth through a gap in his beard. "Some things you can figure though, boys. And right now I would wager that you found your way here by turning to old York for help, right?"

"We sure did," Chic said admiringly. "How'd you ever know that?"

"Can you guess, Fella?"

I could or anybody else that bothered to think about it, but I didn't think Mantus was the kind who would want other people knowing things he was wanting to brag about. "He's the only one that knows where it is?" I asked doubtfully.

Mantus was quite satisfied that I was wrong. "Nothing so simple as that," he assured us. "Jack there serves more than just our crew, you see. There are a number of others who come here for refreshment and relaxation. No, there are a fair number who *could* have told you. The question, then, is how many *would* have told you? Since you are not on intimate terms with any others of Jack's, uh, customers, I naturally conclude that you went back to see York." He was beaming at his own brilliance. It didn't seem all that brilliant to me.

"How would you know who we're close to and who we aren't?" I asked out of a genuine curiosity.

"It is my business to know such things, Fella. After all, an honorable man," he said that part with a gracious little bow of his head, "never interferes with the work or the person of a fellow traveler, you know. It simply is not done."

"Honor among thieves and all that?" I asked.

"Pre*cise*ly, my dear fellow," he said happily. He turned to Chic and laid a stubby-fingered hand on his arm. "I like your partner, Robertson. 'Deed I do." There was something about his voice that I wasn't sure of, a slightly shortened way of saying a word, that sounded almost English to me. "Now if you boys would excuse me, I have to conduct some business with this gentleman." He was referring to the man we hadn't seen before today and who was at the table throughout all that. When Mantus turned away from us, it was as if we no longer existed and wouldn't exist again until he chose to pay some attention to us again.

"C'mon," Chic said. "We better put those horses up for the night."

"Can't we finish this whiskey? It's too good to waste."

"Carry it along then," he insisted. "Ollie's talkin' business here."

"Sure," I said without really meaning it, but I picked up my cup and carried it along behind him.

We turned the horses in with the others where they could get to feed and water and piled our saddles in a tiny shed next to the horse pen. There were more saddles there than there were people we'd seen, but whether there were men to go with them remained to be seen. I figured they could have been spares that were left over from horse-stealing expeditions. Or worse.

Chic didn't want to go back inside the saloon yet, so we sat outside and finished our drinks and waited — me somewhat less patient about it than Chic — until it was coming dark and a few more men began to filter out of the other buildings and into the saloon.

"You can hang around on the doorstep like a potlicker hound if you want," I said finally, "but I'm going inside. It's time we ask where you find some food around here."

Chic came to his feet like somebody'd just tripped loose a spring inside him. He looked annoyed and maybe even angry. "What's that supposed to mean?"

"It means I'm hungry." I guess what I really meant was that I didn't like being here — I'd rather have gotten on those horses and headed for Butte or Bozeman instead of unsaddling — and I wasn't going to take any more of this sitting around and waiting like a kid about to be summoned into a new schoolroom where he'd be the only stranger. And if somebody wanted to mess with me just now, why, that would be fine. It'd give us both something to do.

For a change, it was Chic that backed down. He ducked his eyes away and nodded. "Let's go inside then."

There were a handful of other people in there now, above those who'd been with Mantus earlier. All but one of the men who'd been riding with him that day and two more that I'd not seen before. Those two were paired off in a far corner, and it was plain to see that they weren't part of the Oliver Mantus crowd.

From somewhere out back — which it had to be since we hadn't seen anyone drag it through the front door — Jack Hobarth had produced a big old pot loaded with a good-smelling stew mixture. Those who were interested seemed to be simply dipping from the pot into bowls and providing their own spoons or forks if they had them, gulping it out of the side of the bowl if they hadn't been so farsighted as to bring their own eating tools.

Since we hadn't any warning we tucked in at bowlside and filled up. As stews go, it wasn't bad eating either, but then that is as stews go. As far as I am concerned there isn't a lot of pleasure in any meal you can eat without needing a sharp knife, but then I am prejudiced on that subject. I just plain like red meat and lots of it.

We sat off by ourselves to eat and I imagine Chic was as conscious as me of the inspection we were getting from the others in the room. Nobody was nasty about it in a hard or a challenging way, but they were sure reading everything there was there to see. Of course most of them had already seen us once, just as we'd seen them and could recognize them again now. They would probably know what we were doing here. If the pair in the corner was doing any wondering, though, they were keeping it between them. They were not exactly socializing with the rest.

Not that the Mantus crew was overly

friendly even with each other. They seemed
to be a pretty quiet bunch. Oh, they talked
some, sure. But there wasn't any loud talk
or heavy bragging, and they did their drinking with an air of the bored, long-haul
drinker rather than men having a high time
of it. They were all rough men, but there
sure wasn't any wild behavior here.

After a while the man Mantus had been
talking to got up and left. He wasn't much
more than out of the place before you could
feel a change in the room. Everyone's interest seemed to pick up. They were still quiet
about it, but they talked more. One by one,
the other Mantus men drifted over for a
low-voiced chat with their boss and then
went back to the table where they'd been
sitting.

Once the table was free of people, Jack
Hobarth slipped out the back door and
returned a few minutes later with a towel-
covered tray of food. No common stew pot
for Mr. Mantus, by damn.

The man seemed to enjoy his meal thoroughly. Steak it was and a big one cut thick
and fried to a leathery hue. Later, when the
remains had been cleared away by Hobarth,
he beckoned us over to his table.

"Sit down, boys," he invited. "We'll have
Charlie find you some bunks shortly. In the

meantime I want to have a little talk with you."

We sat, and he went on in a lower voice that wouldn't carry. "Boys," he said, "we have ourselves a job to do soon. We could use your help, and of course you'll be paid very well." He smiled broadly. "You should be happy to hear that this time you'll be paid by the share and not a set amount of money. With any luck at all, the amount could be substantial. Quite substantial indeed."

He sat back and cocked his head and smiled some more, and I would almost swear he was waiting for a rush of gratitude from us new boys. Chic didn't disappoint him.

"We sure 'preciate that," Chic said. "You can count on us t' do our best," he said.

"We'd like to know what it is you want us to do," I said.

Mantus gave an airy wave of his hand. "Oh, don't worry about that. I won't get the details worked out for several days. You will have time to learn what you are to do before the need arises, I can assure you."

That worried me some, but if Chic was bothered he was sure able to avoid showing it. He shook hands with the man named Charlie and chatted with him as we went

271

off to find the bunks we'd be using here. But I sure wasn't easy in my mind. Not about any of this.

CHAPTER 24

Counting Mantus there were four of us. Chic was along, of course, and a man named Taylor, which I believe was his first name though I'm not sure. That is really more of an impression than a fact. Whatever, I never heard more than that one name for him, and I guess it really doesn't matter.

The way Mantus had it figured was pretty clever all right, and it was worked out so that there should be no need for any shooting. He'd made it plain enough why he always tried to arrange things so, when possible.

"The more you shoot, boys, the more you hit. And the more and the harder you put lead into them, the more and the harder they'll come after us afterward, eh? Remember that, boys. The more the blood, the longer the pursuit. So keep your guns quiet if you can. It'll go easier on us if you do," he'd said. Then he'd given the three of us a bent grin. "Hard as that could be," he had added.

So it was pretty clear that he didn't care a whit about those people who would be under his guns, just about how hard it would be to stay clear of trouble once the job was done. Which really was all right by me. I didn't much care what road he wanted to take as long as we both arrived at the same place from it, and it seemed that we did.

What they . . . no, that isn't the honest way to put it. What *we* were going after this time was a pair of speculators who were to be carrying cash on their way to buy a series of claims from some old boys who wouldn't leave their place to meet with the new owners in one of the boom towns. The buyers were to be traveling with two bodyguards and maybe with the engineer who'd done their survey and assay work on the claims. Mantus hadn't said how much they were to be carrying, but it was supposed to be a bunch of money.

We were to take them as they climbed a narrow path under a sheer rock face not too far from the claims. According to Mantus the spot was close enough to the claims that they would have let their guard down some but far enough away that the miners couldn't come out to help them before we could hit and be gone.

Taylor and I were on top of the rocks lying flat so we couldn't be seen. When Mantus gave us the signal, we were to belly forward and simply shove our guns out over the edge. We'd be looking right down on their heads and be able to cover them easily without giving anyone there a shot back at us.

Chic was stationed at the top of the path where he could step out and put a stopper in the bottle at that end. Mantus himself was hiding at the foot of the trail. He would move into the open as soon as they passed and finish the trap from that end.

The surprise and our guns being right over their heads were to keep them quiet. As soon as Mantus had the money we would hold them while he and Chic pulled back afoot. Then Taylor and I could climb up to where we'd left all four horses. I would take my horse and Chic's and go pick him up. Taylor was to circle around and meet Mantus with his horse.

Now I was beginning to wonder if this robbery business was going to be what I expected or if it was going to turn out to be all bragging and waiting, for we sure were doing a bunch of waiting while Taylor was doing a fair amount of bragging, maybe because there just wasn't much of anything else to do while we were hiding on those rocks. It was tiresome and kind of warm there in the afternoon sun, and I was startled to realize it afterward but I started to doze while we waited. Taylor reached over and poked me in the ribs and I tried to pay more attention after that.

We'd been there better than an hour, probably more like two, when they came. We didn't really need the signal from Mantus. The sound of shod hooves on rock was loud enough it would take a deaf man or a passed-out drunk to miss hearing.

Taylor leaned close and whispered, "Don't you go jumpin' the gun now or Ollie'll be all over the both of us. He don't like his plans mussed up, so wait for his signal."

"If we can hear it over the noise of those horses," I told him, but he didn't see any humor in that at all.

The sounds were coming from smack underneath us when Mantus finally whistled from down at the foot of the path.

There wasn't any turning back now. I pulled the old Colt from its scabbard and shoved myself forward to the edge. Damn but it seemed a long way down from our rocks to the path and even farther from there on down the slope. I hadn't noticed that before.

"Set still, gentlemen," Taylor hollered, though we were only a few feet above their heads.

There were five riders on the path. It was easy to see which were the two who were supposed to guard the bodies. They were the ones dressed in sensible clothes and carrying their guns out where they could be got to. The other three were dressed in suits, right down to the ties and gaiters and batwing collars. Each of the five looked to be so scared they couldn't spit.

From where we were, I couldn't see either Chic or Mantus, but Mantus's voice carried up the trail clearly enough.

"You men know what we want," Mantus called. "Pass it over quietly; keep your hands where they belong, and no one gets hurt." Judging from the sound he was walking up the trail as he talked. With the path too narrow here for them to turn their horses, he should be safe enough behind them even at close range. Chic, ahead of them, was in the danger spot. I hadn't thought of that before, but I'll bet Mantus had.

"Dig it out of your pockets now, gentlemen," Mantus said, less loudly now that he was closer. He came into sight from our perch. He had a cocked revolver in each hand and a smiling expression that nevertheless said he would be willing to shoot.

The guard at the rear either knew something about Oliver Mantus or was able to read the willingness to kill that was in his eyes. The man turned back forward in his saddle and told his employers, "He means it, boys, and they got us cold turkey. You'd better hand it over and hope we come out alive, for that's all the choice we got."

One of the better-dressed men, the second from the front just behind the leading guard, leaned out to the side to see around his friends for a better look at Mantus. I could see this man plain, for he was immediately below me. There was intelligence in his eyes and no fear apparent at all. "I agree," he said crisply. "Pointless, of course, to lose more than we must. Give them the money, Donovan." He gave each of us a cold, haughty glare that expressed his opinions more fully than any barrage of cussing could have done.

When his eyes met mine, it was all I could do to keep from sliding back across the ledge to where I couldn't be seen. He turned his stare onto Chic last. Chic was in view now just above and head of them on the path, about on a level with the rocks where Taylor and I lay with drawn guns.

The middle man in the line, who must've been Donovan, unbuckled a flap on his saddle pockets and reached inside. With a sigh that I could clearly hear, he pulled out a thick envelope heavily banded and tied with thongs. He looked at it and hefted it once. "You're sure, Nate?"

"I am," his partner said without hesitation. He hooked a thumb in my direction. "Take a close look at them if you doubt my judgment."

Both Nate and Donovan did, and I felt my face growing warm under their study. I could feel their contempt and disgust flowing across the short distance between us.

"Quit stalling," Taylor growled. He sounded mean as hell, and Donovan flinched and paled but Nate did not.

Donovan threw the packet up to Taylor who made a neat, left-handed catch. Taylor grinned with all the sincerity of a he-wolf and shoved the envelope inside his shirt. "I got it, boss," he called down to Mantus.

"Do you?" Mantus asked. "Open it and make sure." He hefted his revolvers as if he hoped they were trying to run a bluff on him so he could do something about it.

Taylor laid his pistol down on the ledge and unbuttoned his shirt. He rummaged inside for a moment and finally pulled the envelope back into view. With a none-too-sharp belt knife he sawed the thongs apart and riffled through the contents. From where I was I could see too. Gold-backed currency and lots of it. Most places up here would accept that as readily as coin, though you couldn't say the same down home.

"It's money all right, boss," he called. "Just the way it's supposed to be."

I guess my attention and probably Mantus's as well was on Taylor and the sheaf of money he held. Without warning a damp, red socket appeared in Taylor's throat. At the same time there was a soft, almost polite little snap of a small-caliber pistol being fired and a sound when the bullet hit that was not unlike what you get when you thunk a small hatchet into a rotten tree stump. Taylor sprawled forward on the rock.

The shooting startled me so much, I yanked the trigger of my old revolver and cut one loose somewhere in the general direction of the men below me. I wasn't even looking that way at the time and have no idea where my ball might've gone.

I came back to my senses and looked in time to see the fourth man in the line trying to bring his frightened horse back under control on the narrow trail. He had a tiny, rimfire pocket pistol in his hand and the remains of a satisfied and defiant smile on his face. That didn't last long. As I watched he was racked by bullets striking him from both front and rear as Chic and Mantus got into the action.

There was a roll of gunfire like mountain thunder and through the noise I heard Mantus shouting, "Cut the bastards down, boys. Every one of them."

On my hardrock perch I felt almost detached from the whole thing. I sat and watched as the fourth man, who had to be the engineer, slid out of the saddle, and with a loud squeal his horse pitched over the edge to tumble, legs flailing, down the rock-studded slope.

The lead bodyguard went next with one of Chic's bullets in his chest, and Mantus put several into the other bodyguard. That man dropped the gun he'd just gotten into his hand and clutched at his saddle horn.

The lead man's horse was scared too and had nowhere to go but straight ahead. It scrambled up and over — or maybe through — Chic who was on the narrow trail directly in its path. Its near shoulder smashed into Chic and flung him into the rock wall. Somehow it got past without trampling him.

Something exploded near my head and

set my left ear to ringing. The man called Nate — he seemed to be the last of them left now — was staring straight into my eyes. A wisp of smoke was left curling within the open bore of a pistol he was aiming at my face. Coolly he was recocking the thing for another shot.

My own gun was pointed into his chest. We were so close together that I couldn't possibly miss him. I tried to pull the trigger. I really tried. I squeezed on the butt of that gun until my hand shook, but I couldn't pull the right piece of metal.

Nate must've seen it. His gun was cocked again, but he hesitated for a moment and his eyes widened.

I shifted my aim to the side and fired in the desperate hope I could at least make him flinch off target.

It didn't work, but a light of some kind of understanding came into his eyes and he started to open his mouth.

If he was going to say something I will never know what, nor even if that was his intention. A bullet from down the slope plowed into his side. Another hit him from Chic's side of the action, and his eyes glazed. His gun barrel drooped and from somewhere he found the strength to touch off a last shot. A spray of rock dust was flung back into his face, but I'm sure he was beyond feeling it.

Nate fell from his saddle and nearly landed on top of Mantus who somehow had squeezed past the frightened horses below. Mantus was starting to climb the rock face below me but stopped when he saw I was still upright.

"You're all right?"

I nodded.

"Taylor?"

"Done for," I told him. I could barely hear him. My own voice in answer sounded close and hollow as if it was echoing around inside my head without ever being able to get out where it could be heard.

"Throw the money down," Mantus yelled. "You hear me? Get the money. Throw it down to me."

It seemed a sensible idea, and I was glad to know what to do. I shifted sideways. There was a good bit of gore under Taylor and I didn't want to touch him, but I knew I had to.

"What's going on up there? Do you have it? Come on, Fella." Mantus's voice was prodding, insistent.

I touched Taylor's shoulder and felt the flesh give without resistance of any sort. It was an odd sensation and one I did not like.

I shoveled a hand under his shoulder and levered his chest off the rock far enough to see the envelope lying there. By some much appreciated miracle it was still clean and unstained. I reached underneath Taylor and pulled it free.

"Hurry, dammit. Those miners will be coming."

I scooted forward and let the envelope drop heavily into Mantus's waiting hands.

"That's good, Fella. Just right." He sounded and looked quite happy now. He was alone on the path now except for a couple bodies. The horses had all disappeared uphill except for the one the engineer had been riding. I could see it, unmoving, at the foot of the steep slope.

"Go on now, Fella," Mantus instructed. "Just like before. Take Robertson's horse and go on. Leave Taylor's and mine where they are. I'll come around to them. Right?"

I nodded. Chic was nowhere in sight. He'd be expecting me to meet him at the top of the hill. He needed that horse. And that was the direction the miners would be coming from. I picked myself up and began an uphill, hands-and-knees scramble. I didn't want to let Chic down now. Except for that, I really would not have cared.

CHAPTER 25

The customers in Hobarth's place were in a mood to celebrate, and if anyone was grieving for the now departed Taylor they sure were doing a fine job of hiding the fact.

There were more people in residence than we'd seen before, including old York and several others who seemed to be part of the Mantus crowd. Once I began paying some attention to it I got the idea also that there were others, probably several others, we still hadn't met. There were also more outsiders, several riding in that evening as if they somehow had known that the Mantus crew was heavy in the pocket and would be playing host.

A doughtery wagon loaded with painted and powdered and wide-hipped women drove in too and released its cargo into the place like so many hens fluttering out of a too-small coop.

I noticed then — and how it had escaped

my attention before I don't know — that this seemed to be about the only thing at Hobarth's that a man was expected to pay for on his own. Everything else — booze, food, beer, or whatever — you just dipped into and used whenever and to whatever extent you chose. Mantus must've been paying our way, and I guessed that the outsiders must have paid Jack Hobarth at some preset fixed rate, maybe by the day or the week or even the month. However they worked it out I never once saw money change hands from any guest to Hobarth.

This lighter, gayer mood made the place seem quite unlike the quiet, subdued room where we'd spent our time before. Now the voices were raised to carry over or through the cheerful, loud voices of all the others there. Now the men jolted their drinks down between bursts of laughter where before they had sipped slowly over mulled thoughts.

Someone had a harmonica in action and others used the music to provide background for brief spurts of dancing. Brief because no sooner had someone selected a partner and started clomping than he or someone else would haul the darlin' girl outside. Surprisingly, no one showed any offense at these intrusions. It seemed to be understood that the ladies were entitled to earn a living, and they weren't being paid for their dancing.

Mantus was established at his usual table in the corner. It seemed to be his and his alone, with others sitting there only by invitation. He sat and bobbed his head genially to everyone who passed by and drank hot coffee in huge draughts. I'd seen him enjoy his mug of whiskey on other occasions but not this night.

At one time or another during the evening, each of his crowd, me included, was summoned to a chair across the table from him and was paid a share of the take. He never said how much had been in that envelope nor how many shares it was divided into. Nor for that matter how much larger than ours his share was. I do know that he handed me a sheaf of eight fifty-dollar bills for my share and Chic was given the same.

"You boys did nice work today, Fella," he told me when he handed it across, which he did in full view of everyone in the room. "You might want to know that in this organization everyone shares in the profits whether or not he directly participated." He seemed right proud of that when he said it and perhaps it was a marvelously fair and democratic thing among such gangs. I wouldn't know, not having had experience before this.

I nodded and made some noises about how nice that was and shoved the money into a pocket. I didn't really know what else to do with it.

"Yes, Fella, I'm glad I picked you boys up. Your partner is going to be a real asset, I know, and you'll get the hang of things soon enough too." He grinned happily and said, "No joke intended there, Fella. And you will. You did just fine for your first time out."

He reached forward and gave me a friendly whack on the arm. "Don't you worry about a thing now, and remember . . . that bundle in your pocket is just a start. My boys do all right, see? There will be more coming."

"Sure," I told him. He smiled at me with all the tolerant good will of a doting grandfather and then turned his attention elsewhere. It was plain that as soon as he turned away I was no longer part of the world as far as he cared. I found it hard to believe that these other people bought the idea of how concerned he was for them and their welfare, but they sure seemed to. They just thought the world of him and remarked often to each other about what a fine leader he was. They didn't seem to notice or maybe didn't care that Mantus hadn't mentioned nor apparently thought about Taylor once since the man was killed. I shook my head and walked away.

Chic was sitting at a table with Charlie and another man I didn't know. I pulled a chair out and joined them.

"Bert ol' buddy, this's Jonathon, uh, Jackson, uh, Peel," he said drunkenly. "Right, Johnny?"

"Hey now, you remembered all that jes fine, pal. Damn if you din." He seemed pretty well drunk too. It seemed to be in the air tonight.

"From what Ollie says, ol' Chic here is a pretty good ol' boy in a tight," Charlie observed fondly. You would've thought that Chic's odd glory amongst these people was somehow due to Charlie's influence. As far as I know, they had spoken together before for maybe a total of ten minutes, spread over a four-day period between when we arrived and when we went out this morning.

"Have another nip, my friend," Chic offered. He took all the cups from the table and filled them and brought a fresh one for me too. Chic, at least, was in a good mood. And the whiskey was still good.

We partied and I guess we all got pretty drunk, for I lost a good part of the evening so far as knowing what I did during that time. In the morning I was loggy-headed, sour-bellied, and more than a little upset with myself, both for the night before and for the day before. When I woke up Chic was already awake and stirring in the tiny shack we shared. Actually we had half of a building with a solid wall down the middle and doors to the outside from the two separate rooms. Charlie had been sharing the other end with Taylor and now was alone.

"You look like hell with a half hitch tied in its tail" Chic greeted me when he saw I was awake.

I shoved the blankets aside — they needed washing, or maybe burning — and sat up. "That don't make sense," I protested. It was too late to do any good by making myself throw up now, but I sure wished I'd thought of it the night before.

Chic laughed and gave me an elaborate shrug before he went back to his shaving. He made a couple sure-handed strokes that made me shudder just to watch them and playfully nipped the lather at me. It was just luck that he missed. I sure wasn't feeling like ducking.

"Any fool that'd be cheerful on a morning like this oughta be hung," I told him.

"Hell, Bert, we jus' might be hung, too, any ol' time now." He even sounded cheerful about *that*.

What was worse, he was absolutely right. I don't care how you wanted to slice it, if we were taken now we would likely hang. Everything before we just might've explained away, at least a little bit, if we could get someone to believe us. But not now. As far as the law would be concerned now, we were tied smack in with Oliver Mantus and all the things he and his crowd had done in this country. We'd been right there when all those men died. We'd taken a share of the robbery money. We were part and parcel of the whole shebang now.

"You didn't have to bring that up," I told my friend.

"Aw now, Bert," he said more seriously, "I didn't mean it like that. I was jus' playing with you. Hell, you know we ain't done a thing that wasn't forced on us an' never shot at any man that didn't bring it to us." He walked over and clamped a hand on my shoulder. "Don't let it bother you now. You ain't done the first thing to be shamed of."

"Sure," I said. But dammit I *was* ashamed of what we'd done the day before. Not of anything we'd done up until then, no. Deliberately going out and taking part in a robbery, though, was a whole nuther thing.

The odd thing about it though was that even with what we'd done and even with how I felt about it, I still felt like the same person I'd been before. I mean, here I was now, a common criminal and no doubt fair game for anybody who wanted to take us down, and at the same time I still felt as strong as ever that the laws are meant to be kept, if only because they are what keeps people being more or less fair and peaceable with one another. So now I didn't really know what to think or do.

I knew I'd rather saddle up and do some wandering and try to forget about this, but I also knew I never could. And as cheerful as Chic was being this morning, I was wondering if he would even want to forget it if he was given the chance.

"What do you think about that money Mantus gave us yesterday?" I asked him outright.

"Yeah, ain't that something," he said happily. He sure had missed my meaning on that one. "Boy, Bert. Talk about easy money. Ollie sure knows how to come up with it, doesn't he?" He reached into his pocket and pulled out a wad of currency. He fanned the bills to admire them. "Isn't that great? A few more like this an' I c'n go back and do some serious talkin' to Elaine."

I couldn't hardly believe what I'd just heard. "Good God, Chic! You'd go back to that girl with dirty money in your pocket and the law on your neck?"

"Oh, she needn't know about any of this. It ain't like either of us would ever tell her. We could just go somewhere else an' it'll be all right. Hell, it isn't like there's so many around that'd recognize us once we're away from here. Or even if we stayed here, for that matter."

Well, there wasn't much I could say to that. I pulled my pants on and got out of there without waiting to wash or shave or anything else.

Elaine Beasley deserved better than either Chic or me. I had to find some way to show him that.

CHAPTER 26

Mantus did not keep us or any others of his crowd exactly busy, but he always had something in the works. A whole lot more than I would have wanted, had it been up to me. I didn't like any part of it.

Not that all of it was so bad by itself. Once he had us go with Charlie and Jon Peel and a couple boys who weren't part of the crowd. We went up into Montana and met some men who were night-driving a small herd of cattle. Charlie gave them a few dollars a head for the cows and we brought them back into the hills where Mantus could sell them to the beef-hungry miners at extra-high prices. Everybody got hundred-dollar shares for that, and for a change it was work I enjoyed. Lordy, but it was nice to be back at the rump end of some bovines again for a few days, even if they were stolen cattle. We also ate pretty well after that as we held out a handful of them for our own use, everyone pitching in to build another pen to hold them. I was kind of interested to see that these were blockier, heavier, shorter-legged cattle than I was used to. Someone said they likely came from Oregon, and I could not disagree.

Another time we were handed a hundred fifty dollars apiece as a share for something that had gone on while Mantus was away for a few days. I never did hear where that money had come from, and I never asked.

He had Chic and me take some horses down to York's place once and leave them in his pen. York wasn't there at the time, which pleased me just fine. It felt good to be away from that crowd for a time.

"How much money do you have squirreled away now?" I asked Chic while we were down there.

He looked at me once and gave out with a healthy laugh. "Bert ol' buddy, I know as good as you do what you're fixing to ask. You been tippytoein' around it ever since we got to Hobarth's. Well the answer is that it ain't enough."

"I've got some too, you know. Between us maybe —"

"No," he cut me off. "An' that's the end of it, see?" He was even starting to talk like

Mantus now. "Ollie's been good to us, an' you know it. We c'n hang in with him a while longer."

"Chic, what is it you *want*? Just what in hell do you want, anyway?"

He stood in his stirrups and practically yelled, "I want —" He clamped his mouth shut. He shook his head and said, "Oh hell, Bert. I don't know. Not now, huh? Please?"

What could I say? I nodded and crawled down off the horse I was riding, which this time was an ugly blue roan that looked awful but turned out to have a whole bunch of bottom. Chic followed me into the shack and began rummaging through the stuff on the shelves to see what we might be having for dinner.

After we got back from York's place, Mantus sent the two of us over west into Wyoming to the Belle Fourche where we were to wait at a particular place to meet a man and guide him back to Hobarth's. If he didn't show up in four days, we were to come back. He didn't show.

We lay around for another week, eating and loafing and sampling Hobarth's wares, all courtesy of Oliver Mantus. It was about then that I realized how much I'd taken to drinking of an evening and cut back to an occasional beer. And that was when, with

me sober, I saw how much Chic was drinking here. I hadn't really noticed it before,
and he was always in a fine mood in the
mornings these days. Now it began to worry
me. It was the same every night, and he
never seemed to see anything unusual in it
And there wasn't a thing I could do about
it

About the end of that week, another man
arrived who was a member of the crowd but
who we hadn't exactly met yet. Not, at least,
as a part of the same crowd we were running with, though I had sure seen him
before this. It was that same Roy that I'd
had a fight with back in Deadwood. He was
cleaned up now, his hair and mustache
trimmed and clean shaven, but I had no
trouble recognizing him. It seemed he
remembered me too.

He saw me and Chic at one of the tables
as soon as he came in. His eyes narrowed
and he missed a beat in his walking. He had
been headed toward Mantus's table, but he
swerved aside to come toward us. He began
showing that cocksure, nasty grin as he got
close to the table.

"You got a habit of picking the wrong
place to stop for a beer, fella," he said. His
grin got wider and nastier. "I sure am glad
about that."

"Now it's real fine to hear you say that, Roy, for I always like to see a man be pleased about things. Any time it would please you to see was that first go-round a fluke, why, I'll be happy to oblige you there too." I guess my hackles were starting to raise the same way his seemed to be.

We might have got something going up again except that Mantus's voice cut across the room with a sharp, "Roy!" That one word was enough. Roy stabbed me good and hard with his eyes but he turned away and hurried to his boss's table where they huddled in a low-voiced conversation.

"What was that all about?" Chic wanted to know.

So I told him. I'd been marked enough that last time that Chic knew I'd been in a scrap but we'd never gotten into any detail about it before.

"If you whupped him, you'd better keep an eye on him now," Chic said. "He looks like a bad one."

Which was kind of a strange thing for Chic to say here. There wasn't a good one in the lot at Hobarth's, and by this time I wasn't sure that I would want to except even Chic and me from that statement. It just wasn't a place where the better element was going to be found.

"I guess I'll have to," I agreed.

Roy finished his talk with Mantus and drew himself a cup of whiskey. He gave me a hard look but carried his drink to a table as far away from us as he could get. I watched him settle and turned back to see Mantus motioning to me to join him, which I did.

"Yes?"

"Sit down, Fella. Good. Have a drink?"

I shook my head, and Mantus smiled his approval.

"Garret tells me you two have had some trouble in the past," Mantus said, coming right to the point.

"Garret. That would be Roy, I take it."

"Roy Garret. Yes. And a fine man, Fella. You might remember that, see? He might be regarded as my second in command if we had such a thing, which we do not. Still, he is a highly able and highly valuable member of our organization. I have already reminded him, however, and now wish to warn you." The phony smile slid off his face. "I will allow no personal feelings to interfere with our work here. Absolutely no feuding. One man is not required to like another, but you are expected to work together. You do understand this?"

I nodded.

"Good. See that you remember it. Garret has a tendency toward a spot of the high temper now and then. Deplorable of course, but there it is. Should you feel yourself provoked, I will expect you to walk away," he ordered. "Quietly. Regardless of your own inclinations, you see? I will expect that of you, Fella. And above all, there will be *no* knife or gun work here. The penalties would be *quite* severe."

"It sounds like you're laying the biggest burden on me, Mantus," I told him outright. I figured I might as well have my side of it understood right up front too. "If you want me tame, you'd best put just as short a leash on him."

"Fair enough as far as it goes," he said, "but remember what I told you, yes?"

I shrugged. "As far as it goes, sure."

"Fine," he said, and the interview was over. Later on he called Chic over and I suppose gave him a warning to watch me. I didn't especially like that, but Chic never mentioned what was said and so there wasn't much for me to bluster about.

If I'd been uncomfortable around the place before, I was doubly so now. Whenever Roy Garret and I were in the same room I could feel the hate coming out of him. Whenever we were in sight of each other he was watching me. And in truth I was watching him just the same way.

To make it worse, the others in the crew — Jon Peel and Charlie and a pair of brothers named Eric and Lonnie something-or-other and a couple more whose names I can't remember — seemed to think that Roy Garret was the toughest and the swellest ol' boy there ever was, next to Oliver Mantus. I don't know what they thought this was all about. I sure never discussed it with any of them, but there was no doubt whose side of it they were taking. They froze us out cold.

Personally I didn't give a damn about them or their company to start with and wasn't going to start caring now. It did seem to bother Chic, though, and of course he got it too as we were lumped together.

The day after Garret arrived, Mantus sent one of the boys off somewhere. He was gone three days, and when he came back he had a long, private conversation with his leader. That evening Mantus invited most everybody for those one-by-one talks he seemed to favor.

The upshot of it was that the next morning there were people riding in all directions. What all the rest of them were doing I didn't know, although some of it became obvious later on.

Anyway, Chic and I were in the party that rode with the great man himself, along with Jon Peel and the Aaron brothers. That was their name. Who could ever forget a name like Eric Aaron? Anyway, they were along and so was Garret and a man named Bumper. It was an awful big group and had to mean something special was afoot.

We rode east carrying along a pack horse loaded with eatables and avoiding Deadwood and the smaller camps where we otherwise might've stopped. We circled east around the edge of the hills and turned south for several days through open country. Never once did Mantus push the horses, staying always to an easy pace that could've been increased a lot more had there been any hurry. Wherever we were going, he seemed to know exactly when he wanted to get there and had allowed plenty of time for doing it.

As it was he brought us eventually to a dandy little hollow out in the exact center of nowhere with wood and water and privacy, just the ideal sort of thing a man looks for when he is wanting to locate a line camp where he can pass the seasons in the most comfort. Yet from the empty country aroundabout you wouldn't know it was there unless you rode right up onto it.

We stopped there and spent the next full day loafing in three separate groups. Mantus stayed off by himself. Chic and I had a patch of shade to ourselves. And the rest of them bunched together around the coffee pot. There wasn't any liquor in with the supplies, and if anyone had brought a private stock he was keeping it to himself. Another of Mantus's rules, I supposed, though no one had ever gone and explained it as such.

He had us awake early the next morning, hurried us through breakfast without seeming to do so, had everything packed and ready to go in short order, and then kept everyone sitting and waiting for nearly an hour while he consulted with his watch. Finally he put the thing back into his pocket and gave us the nod.

We rode south for three hours to another staging area, waited there past the dinner hour, and set off again about three o'clock. I couldn't help notice that someone had passed by this place some time before we arrived. I did not believe that this was by accident. Mantus had somehow known about it and planned for it.

A half hour of brisk riding brought us to the empty railroad tracks. As we got up to them, with not a thing in sight east or west but the lines of silver-rubbed steel, Mantus looked at his watch again and gave a satisfied nod.

"All right, boys," he said, "the last eastbound is past. We have a half hour to tear up some track. Let's get to it."

That part about "let us" do the work proved to be "let you" do the work while Mantus directed, but then I shouldn't have expected different. We all crawled off our horses — I was on that good blue horse again — and the rest of us set about loosening one rail. As poor as the ballast and the bed were along here, we had no real problem with it, and well before Mantus's time limit, we had the rail loose and curled so that it stuck plainly into the air. Any engineer who wasn't asleep could not avoid seeing the broken track ahead of him.

"Follow me now," Mantus ordered, and it was back onto the horses for everyone.

I hadn't noticed it before, but there was a fold in the rolling grass not more than a couple hundred yards away, and Mantus took us right to it and into it.

"This is deep enough that we won't be seen from the train," he explained, "as long as we remain dismounted. We will not go to the train until I signal. Remember that. Not until I tell you. We will wait while they stop and prepare for an attack. We will wait while they repair the track. When they have relaxed their suspicions, I will give you the word and we will go forward. Not until then. Remember this."

Mantus proceeded to tell us each where to go and what to expect and what to do in return. There was something for everyone to be doing. The Aaron brothers were to hold the crew at the front of the train. Chic and I had the caboose and the brakemen there. Jon Peel and Bumper were to take a collection from the passengers. Mantus and Garret would hit the mail car. I noticed that everyone was doubled up. In case any one man was shot, I figured. I noticed too that the Aaron boys were told *not* to get any bright ideas about telling the train crew to pull their fires. The train was to be allowed to keep its steam.

Well, it worked just about as smooth as it was planned. We hid. The train arrived. They stopped in plenty of time to avoid a wreck, took a while staying inside to talk it over and finally got out to fix the bent rail. Only when they had it done and the crew was fixing to get back aboard did Mantus say we could go.

We all mounted and went larruping toward the train and had them under our guns pretty much before they knew what was up.

I only heard one shot fired as we approached and that was by one of our group. Later, while Chic and I were enjoying a cup of coffee from the crew-quarters stove and joking with the three brakemen, there was another, single shot from somewhere forward in the cars. Within ten minutes, we heard Mantus yelling for everyone to get out.

It was that easy. Bing-bang, and away we go. We followed him back into the same depression where we'd waited before and damned if he didn't have us dismount again.

"We'll wait here while they decide we've gone and get rolling again," he said. "Then we cross back over and ride north."

Jon and Bumper each had cloth sacks full of cash taken from the passengers. Nothing else was taken. Cash only, by Mantus's order. And Garret had a pair of larger canvas sacks that were made bulky by something inside them. Something that wasn't too awful heavy and so almost had to be currency. These were tied one behind Mantus's saddle and one behind Garret's.

The train belched smoke and hissed and clanked and began rolling forward.

"Won't they be after us awful quick?" I couldn't help asking.

Mantus must've been in a good humor, for he smiled and nodded and even bothered to answer me.

"Early enough to have more than an hour of daylight for tracking when they return here," he said. "They will know they can rest their horses overnight, so they will race after us in the hope of overtaking us before dark. This they will not do, but they will try. When they stop their mounts will be very tired, you see." He smiled again. "Then, you see, *we* will find *them*. Entirely too far from the railroad to easily walk back, flag a train, and reorganize a pursuit. With luck we should not again be bothered by pursuit this time."

Mantus looked quite triumphant. So did Roy Garret. At first I thought this was because of his boss's planning, but then I noticed how Garret seemed to keep looking my way with a quiet, cunning, ugly little smile.

Well, I might've been finding the kind of boogers there that frighten a spooky horse, but all the same I began to wonder about that and to worry.

And the more I thought about it the more it made sense. We would be going into a nighttime fight with that posse. Whether directed mostly at them or at their horses it made little difference about one thing. There would be a lot of shots going off in the dark, and who could say what shot hit which man at a time like that? If Garret accidentally shot me, it would be just too bad. Or good. There would be fewer shares to be paid out of the take.

The more I thought about it, the more convinced I was that I was right. And the more worried. And there wasn't anything I could do but continue to ride north with this crowd. Anything else would be certain to end in a hanging. Or maybe something quicker.

CHAPTER 27

My first thought was to drag Chic off to the side and warn him to keep an eye on Garret. I had plenty of opportunity to do just that, for Mantus stopped us in a protected little nest of rocks well before sundown, and again Chic and I were left off by ourselves while the others clustered around the coffee pot. We could pour from it as often as we wanted, but it was plain we were not wanted in the conversation there.

Anyway, we took our coffee and wandered out to where we could see the country around us. We settled where we could lean comfortably back against a standing slab of red rock. It felt cool against my back and, for a time, I just sat there and listened to my belly growl. Mantus had said we wouldn't eat until later. He didn't explain any further, but I was willing to bet he was thinking about belly wounds.

"You're bein' awful quiet," Chic said after

a few minutes. "What's so important that you ain't fussing about bein' hungry?"

I almost told him then, but I did not. I'd been reluctant to say anything and now I realized why. This was my catfish, and it was up to me to clean it and cook it.

And — hidden somewhere back there — I was wondering if I could really count on Chic's help this time. He was so awful high on Mantus and this crowd of his, and he was so high on the idea of putting together a bigger pile of their kind of money, that this time I was afraid to say anything, even to Chic.

"Nothing," I mumbled.

"I don't guess I b'lieve that," he said, "but we'll let it stand."

"Suit yourself," I told him. I drank off the last of my coffee and found that it had gotten too cold. "Yuck."

Chic tasted what he had left, made a face, and then grinned. "Pretty awful, ain't it?" He got to his feet and took my cup. "Wait here. I'll get us some fresh."

That sort of thing sure didn't help the mad I was halfway building for him. It just reminded me of what a good friend he was and what I owed him. Lord knows I owed him enough.

There was the question too, though, of

whether it might be awful unfair to Chic if I told him about my fretting. Even if he didn't take my worries straight to Mantus, even if he did everything he could to help, I might just be dragging him into trouble if I told him what I thought. The rest of the crowd seemed to lump Chic in with me because we were partnered, but, as far as I could tell, Roy Garret had no particular mad on with Chic. Yet Garret would be strong enough to pull the others with him if it came to a fight. And I sure couldn't imagine Oliver Mantus caring one way or the other as long as it didn't interfere with what he wanted now that the job was done.

Chic came back with the fresh coffee, but he looked kind of down. "Something ain't right," he said. "Those boys are edgy as a Green River knife. That damn fool Roy Garret said something about stayin' away from you tonight. Said I oughta stick close to Ollie. What's goin' on here, Bert?"

So I told him.

"Aw hell, is that all?" he asked. The silly bastard was grinning again. "We c'n take care o' that no sweat. Come on." He set his coffee cup aside and stood up.

"Sit down," I tried to tell him, but he wasn't listening. "*Will* you please —" Old Chic was just marching straight away. All I could do was get up and follow him.

Chic took himself smack over to where Garret and the others were gathered in their tight, quiet little circle. Chic stood before Garret and smiled down at him.

"We got a problem, Roy," he said.

"You want me to cry about your problems now?" Garret asked.

"Well," Chic said — he grinned and scratched behind his left ear — "this time maybe you oughta, because you seem to be it."

Garret got to his feet.

"You see," Chic went on, "my ol' partner here, an' me, have got the idea you figure to backshoot him, an' maybe me, when the lights go out t'night. We wouldn't hardly want you t' do that. An' I figured maybe the best thing is t' make sure you don't by us havin' it out now, you see. You do see the sense in that, don't you?"

Garret began to color with anger, but whatever he would've said he had to swallow instead. From behind us came the distinct — and awfully loud — sound of a pair of heavy shotgun hammers being rolled back to cock.

"If you start it, I finish it," Mantus said. I hadn't even noticed him being nearby when we walked over here, but he sure was now.

"You know better than this, Garret. And you had best learn it, Robertson. I will allow none of this now. If you wish, you can take it up later, but not now."

"That doesn't solve our problem, Ollie," Chic protested. It was the first time I'd ever heard him disagree with Mantus. "This weasel c'n do what he wants durin' that scrap tonight, an' later will be just too damn late."

"Garret?"

"Hell, Ollie, you know I'll do whatever you say is best."

"Quite good enough for me," Mantus said. He let the hammers of the shotgun down and set the ugly weapon aside.

"It ain't enough for me," Chic said. His voice was quietly insisting. "Bert an' me ain't riding against that posse tonight with Garret in the crowd."

Mantus began to redden. "How *dare* you?"

"It's not like that, Ollie," Chic said quickly. "Bert an' me can just ride off. We'll do it right now, an' no hard feelings, see?"

"We are not going to count and divide our take with the law on its way," Mantus said.

"All right," Chic returned. "Keep it. We ride away. Now. An' no hard feelings. A man can't be fairer than that."

313

Nor could he. And for Chic Robertson to say such a thing. It was more than I could have expected from him and what I'd been wanting all this while.

"No." Mantus wasn't willing to give an inch to anyone.

Garret was grinning openly. I was willing to bet I knew what he was thinking. He gave me a wink and tickled the butt of his revolver with his fingertips. Well, it was nice to know I'd been dead right — so to speak — after all.

Chic shrugged. "You don't leave us a helluva lot of choice, Ollie."

"Nonsense," Mantus said. He was frowning. He looked as if he simply could not believe that someone was refusing his orders.

"Tell me, Bert. D'you think you can handle Mr. Garret?"

"I did it once," I said. "No reason why I can't again."

"Not much t' do then but go at it," Chic said mildly.

His gun was in his hand and Chic was blowing holes in Oliver Mantus's middle before anyone else had time to blink, including, I think, Oliver Mantus.

Garret was as shocked as the rest of them. He stood staring, immobile, while he watched Mantus go down. That in truth is the only thing that allowed me to get my revolver out ahead of him. It was already cocked and leveled before Garret knew what was going on.

Still he tried. I watched him across my sights while his hand dipped and hooked. It seemed I had all the time in the world to watch this and to wonder if I would be able to shoot a living man even now when I had to or I surely would go down myself.

Garret's gun came up, his thumb pulling on the hammer and the cylinder spinning to line a cartridge under the pin even before it cleared the leather. The muzzle swept out toward my belly. It seemed to move very slowly.

I fired. This time I squeezed and the hammer fell and the old Colt bellowed. I fired square into Roy Garret's chest. Immediately I felt weak and sick. If I'd had to fire again, I could not have done it, but the one ball I did get off, and it was enough. The soft lead ball took him square and sat him down and he was out of the game for good.

My ears were ringing, as much with dizziness as with noise, and the smell of burnt powder was sharply sour in my nose. I could practically taste the heavy acid odor it was so strong, as strong right then as powder smoke in a closed room.

The dizziness began to clear, and I shook my head and looked around. Chic was lying on the ground, but he did not look to be hurt. He had Mantus's shotgun in his hands and had it trained on the others. As far as I could tell none of the other boys had moved.

"Can you cover these birds?" Chic asked.

I sure hell hoped they wouldn't do anything that would make me have to shoot. I didn't think I could. But I wasn't going to let them know that. "You bet," I told him. I waved my revolver muzzle at them in my very best imitation of a really tough killer.

They bought it just fine. They sat like so many wooden Indians while Chic got to his feet.

Chic aimed the scattergun at them again and said, "Boys, the safest thing for you t' do is the same thing we're gonna. Leave us be an' run like hell. That posse is comin' and they may've been close enough to hear the shooting. You don't have Ollie now t' do your planning, so I'd say we all had best cut an' run." None of them said a word in return.

Chic wasn't quite through yet, and I guess he couldn't help thinking about it. He backed off to where Mantus had been sitting earlier and helped himself to the two big, canvas sacks that'd been taken from the UP train. The little bags of money taken from the passengers he left. Maybe he thought he was doing those other boys a favor.

"Get our horses, Bert. An' Ollie's and Garret's too. We'll want spares along, for we're gonna be moving fast."

I did as he said and within a few minutes we were ready to go.

"We won't do you dirt, boys," Chic told the crew still sitting around the dying fire — where no one had wanted to move to add fresh chips when it started to burn low. "We'll leave your horses alone. We won't go off an' leave you no chance with the laws. But, boys, if you ride our way you'll have shooting behind you and before, for if we see you we shoot. Now y'all set still while we get on our way, then you take your own chances."

Jon Peel nodded. No one else moved.

We backed our horses until we had some solid rock between us and the used-to-be Mantus crew. Then we turned and rode like hell.

The posse Mantus had planned on was back there. We could feel them behind us as sure as if they had somehow reached forward and laid weights across our shoulders. For the better part of two weeks, we dodged and ran and pushed those horses and prayed they would hold out and thanked our stars that Chic had thought to bring those spares.

Mantus had probably stashed those extra-good Kentucky horses somewhere nearby to use after the robbery, but we hadn't any idea where they might be. Nor were we interested in taking the time to look for them.

In all that time and all that running, we never once caught actual sight of the posse, and as far as we knew they never got a look at us. Which was just fine by us. It was bad enough being able to feel them back there without having to duck their bullets too.

The feeling of them back behind us disappeared eventually, but we kept going anyway. At the end of the two weeks we were back down in the Cherokee Strip not too far from where the OX5 had been running those steers. Lordy, but that seemed a long time ago. A lot longer than it was.

We made ourselves a camp in a plum thicket. It was a comfortable enough place, even a pretty one, and I could not account for the black mood I was in. Even a proper fire built of sweet-smelling wood instead of cow or buffalo chips did not help. Maybe

I'd somehow seen what was building in Chic's mind. I really couldn't say.

After supper that night we were sitting around picking our teeth and getting ready to sack out when Chic casually said, "I'll bet before long I can slip back up to Cheyenne, Bert. 'Cept this time I'll go in style. Take the train in. Get me a new suit. A new hat. Hit the barber for a bath and a shave an' go a-calling."

I felt myself go cold inside. "You aren't going to do that, Chic."

"What?" He was half smiling, as if he thought I'd made a joke but wasn't quite sure.

"I said you aren't going to do any of that, Chic. You aren't going calling on Elaine Beasley. Not now. Not ever."

He got to his feet. "Why not?" he demanded coldly.

It just didn't make any difference to me any more. Friend or no, fast or no, it just didn't make any difference.

"You and me, Chic. We're neither one of us any good now. We neither of us is fit to step into the same room with that girl. I won't let you do it, Chic."

"You *what*? *You* won't let *me* do what I want? Dammit, Bert, I c'n swat you like a fly an' you know it." He was still more unbelieving than angry.

I felt bone weary. "I know you can, Chic. If it comes to that, I guess you will. But I wouldn't go easy. And I'll still stop you. I swear I will, Chic."

"B'God, you mean it."

"Yes, I do. I mean every word of it. An' neither one of us is going back to Cheyenne. That's just the way it is."

Chic shook his head. He seemed to forget the anger that had been rising inside him. He slumped back onto the ground.

After a minute he raised his eyes and looked at me. "How d'you figure we can go on ridin' together after you saying a thing like that?"

I felt like I was frozen inside and was more listening to my own voice than I was directing it. "I don't figure it, Chic. We got to stop here." I paused to collect what few thoughts I could before I went on. "I know what'll happen, Chic. You've got it in you now. Maybe I have too, but if I do I'll fight it tooth and toenail before I'll ever give in to it. But not you. You'll go back to robbing, Chic. You'll rob people again, and sometime — sooner or later it'll happen — sometime you'll have to kill someone again, and when you do it will be someone with more right to live than either you or me.

"Well I can't do that, Chic. Not again I can't. I won't be able to even forget what we've done up till now. I can't wipe that out, but I can damn well make sure it doesn't happen again."

"You mean every word of that, don't you?"

"I do. Every word."

Chic sat staring into the fire, and after a while, a time that seemed to go on forever, I got up and saddled the ugly blue roan.

"Don't forget your share of the money," Chic said without looking up.

"Thanks. I almost forgot." I dug into my pocket and pulled out what I had left from our earlier shares. I folded the bills into a loose bundle and dropped them onto the ground beside him. He didn't say anything.

I never saw Chic Robertson after that night. I heard early the next year that he was cut down by a small-town Kansas marshal while he was trying to rob some little cheesebox of a bank.

Me, I have a new name now and a beard and a job tending beeves in a lonesome part of Arizona. I have those and a lot of memories and nearly as many regrets. But do you know? Somehow I still keep hoping that one of these days I'll be able to forget. Or that someday I'll be found out and made to pay for what I helped to happen. I'm really not sure which I want more.

ABOUT THE AUTHOR

Frank Roderus wrote his first story at the age of five. A newspaper reporter for nine years, he now lives in Florida where he raises American quarter horses and pursues his favorite hobby, researching the history of the American West. His previous books were *Journey to Utah, The 33 Brand,* and *The Keystone Kid.*